The Treasure Hunter's Daughter

Margot Deguet Delury

Front and back cover images by Madeline Menkes.
ISBN: 9798634068466

TO MY MOTHER, JANE

Thank you for the impromptu road trips and summer reading assignments, the art museum tours and writing prompts. And thank you for warning me not to write a novel, and then hopping onboard as my editor and cheerleader as soon as I decided to anyway.

ACKNOWLEDGEMENTS

I would first like to thank my teacher, Mrs. Rebecca Mlinek, without whose tireless editing and constant support I would not have been able to write this book. Thank you to my sister, Rose, who, at thirteen years old, is already an incredibly astute editor and all-around amazing human being. Thank you to my stepfather, Don, and stepmother, Holly, for their loving support. Finally, I would like to thank my parents, Jane and Anton, who have always, in their own ways, encouraged me to dig past the petunias to find gold.

PIER
ADELSON HOUSE
BANK'S FAMILY ESTATE
WIDE AL'S
MAIN STREET
GIL'S
PARADISE TOWN LIBRARY
THE SWAMPS
PARADISE FUNERAL HOME
WELCOME TO PARADISE, NORTH CAROLINA

Prologue: The Bankses of Paradise, from 1842 to 1995

Nestled in the thickets of the North Carolina coastline is a town named Paradise. It contains five hundred inhabitants, thirty-two rows of neon-painted beach houses, and one supermarket. The town was founded by a man named Thomas Banks, who retreated to the coast in the 1840s to live a life of seclusion. He'd made a fair chunk of money drawing maps of previously unchartered parts of the West Coast, and he used it to build a colonial house in the middle of a marshy swamp.

Back then, the shallow blue tides and moss-webbed trees really did seem paradisiacal to someone like Thomas Banks, who enjoyed taking long, bare-footed walks along the beach and writing poetry about seagulls. But soon, the calls of the seagulls were drowned out by workers beating railroad tracks into the land, and then by the howls of incoming trains. The trains offloaded vacationing families, lumber for houses, and all of the vices of modern society that Thomas Banks had tried to escape. Paradise became a premiere vacation spot. The mossy swamp trees were cut down to make room for new homes. The trunks were stripped of their limbs and pounded into the ocean floor to support a fishing pier.

Then came the great hurricane of 1854, which ravaged the town, pummeling the new pier, flooding houses, cluttering the beach with debris. Vacationers left as quickly as they had come, retreating to the safe center of the country and leaving Thomas Banks to bemoan the destruction of his paradise. According to his diary entries, which are now yellowing in a shelf in the Paradise Library, Banks believed that the storm was God's way of punishing the townspeople for ruining Paradise. He died alone in his bed at the age of forty-five, leaving his wife and daughter with a room full of maps, a house on the beach, and a pessimistic view of society.

This view, it seems, was passed down through generations. Banks' daughter, Evelyn, bought out the entirety of the swamps next to the Banks estate, and was known to yell at children who played there. She refused to marry, and raised her son, Earnest, under the Banks name and without a father. Earnest left the home as soon as his mother died, favoring instead the life of a farmer in the Midwest. The estate became decrepit under his ownership. The lovely wrap-around porch started to cave in on itself as the damp wood became infested with moss and families of mice. The shingles fell off one by one, worn by the deluge of summer rains that Paradise was known for.

Earnest's children similarly ignored their Paradise estate, and it wasn't until Earnest's grandson, Gordon, came of age that the house was finally revisited. Gordon Banks aspired to be the single most prominent architect of the 1930s. He had married into a wealthy family, and decided to use his wife's fortune to demolish Thomas Banks' colonial home and replace it with a large Spanish-style mansion, fitted with clay tiles, a stucco facade, and a crushed gravel drive. Gordon and his wife moved into the house after four years of construction and gave birth to their first and only son, Randolph "Randy" Banks.

Randy Banks grew up to be much like his great-great-great grandfather, Thomas Banks. He majored in cartography at the local community college, he was prone to taking walks along the beach and reading poetry, and he rarely interacted with the other members of the town. And when, at sixty-three years old, he passed away in an anonymous room in Paradise Hospital, he was entirely alone.

Chapter One: The Seashell

Three blocks away from the Banks estate, a girl named Jade Adelson sat on the brim of the ocean and listened to the clangs of her grandmother's wind chimes. The sun was still pulling itself up from the horizon, rays stretched out to hook onto the drifting clouds. The water trailed between her toes lazily, sucking in and then out as if it were breathing. Jade watched it with a mind almost completely devoid of thought, which was unusual for her. It was the first day of summer break, and she had nothing to do except watch the ocean breathe.

Jade and her grandmother, Margaret, had moved to Paradise fifteen years before, when Jade was only six months old. As Paradise was a small town, there was a great deal of gossip surrounding their arrival. Who were Jade's parents and why weren't they there, and why had Margaret left her busy life as a New York City big-press editor to come here? The rumors only increased in circulation as people became acquainted with Margaret.

The first unusual thing about Margaret was her house. Soon after purchasing the chipping baby-blue house on the shoreline, Margaret bedecked the ocean-facing side with wind chimes. There were your average wind chimes, dripping with beads and ringing metal tubes, but there were also wind chimes made of blown glass, old CDs, and even animal bones. Right by the front door hung Margaret's favorite possession: a ceramic bird wind chime with bells and real bird feathers. The bird's beak had broken off when it fell onto the porch during a storm, but it still hung, wounded, eyeing visitors as they knocked on the door.

As there was a great deal of wind on the beach, the wind chimes were always clashing amongst and against each other, creating a discordant symphony which soon upset the neighbors. Mrs. Next Door, a retiree from Georgia whose name Margaret never bothered to learn, went straight to the house on Margaret's second day in Paradise and demanded that she take the wind chimes down. Margaret shut the door in Mrs. Next Door's face and the bird wind chime swung precariously.

Jade didn't question her grandmother's wind chimes. She had grown used to their sounds, just as she'd grown used to the rest of her grandmother's quirks. The newspaper clippings and bird paintings all along the orange-painted walls, the Italian opera resounding from the living room, the way her grandmother whispered poems under her breath while she cooked. Back in elementary school, she'd felt a tinge of embarrassment every time she brought a friend home. Margaret was hopeless at setting up playdates; she missed every PTA meeting and always rubbed Jade's friends' mothers the wrong way.

"My mom thinks your grand-mom is *weird*," one girl confided to Jade in the elementary school cafeteria.

Then, on the second day of sixth grade, Jade sat next to a girl named Lily Treen. Lily's dad owned Paradise's rundown bar, Wide Al's, and her mom was infamous throughout the school for having dated the principal and half of Lily's teachers. Just like Margaret, Lily's mom didn't braid hair before school or pack lunches with little notes tucked into the seams. She didn't chaperone class field trips to the beach or go on power-walks with the rest of the school moms. And when she dropped Lily off for a sleepover a week later, she stayed to have a drink with Margaret.

Jade was thinking about the beginnings of her friendship with Lily on this particular day, as she felt the ocean tug at the damp sand around her feet. Ever since she found out about old Randy Banks' death, she'd been thinking a lot about her life and the people in it. Margaret had just turned sixty that month, so she was just a few years younger than Randy had been.

"Jay!" Turning to see her grandmother walking across the sand in her favorite blue-and-white striped bathing suit, Jade was reminded that Margaret was no average sixty-year old.

"How's the water?" Margaret asked, pulling her swim cap farther down her scalp.

"Not bad!" Jade called out, smiling and splashing her foot down on the thin layer of water.

Margaret walked in slowly. "Liar!" she exclaimed, turning back to her granddaughter. "It's freezing." But she lowered herself into the water nonetheless, walking further and further into the cold surge until Jade could only see her white swim cap floating above the current. "Are you coming in?" Margaret called, her breathing heavy from treading.

"No," Jade said, standing up and brushing the sand off of her knees. "I'm getting some breakfast. Want anything?"

"I'm good here," Margaret said, letting her feet float up so that she was lying across the water, her stomach pushed up to stay afloat. She called out as Jade turned back to the house. "Remember, we have to be at the funeral home at twelve!"

Jade shook her head as she walked back to the house, sand clotting between her toes. She wiped her feet on the mat outside the door, grabbed a peach off of the kitchen counter, and ran up the two flights of stairs to her room. Jade lived in the attic. She loved the low, arched ceiling, the feeling of having a whole floor to herself. It didn't hurt that Margaret was afraid the attic was haunted, so she rarely ever braved the last set of stairs. This was Jade's space, where she could lie down on her bedspread, suck the last of her peach from its pit, and wonder why on Earth Margaret insisted on spending the first day of summer break attending Randy Banks' funeral.

On the day that Randy died, Margaret came back from the grocery store in a state. Crying as she shoved a carton of milk into the fridge, Margaret had explained to Jade that Randy had been her first friend in Paradise. They'd grown apart over the years, but Margaret still took his death personally.

Jade threw the cracked peach pit into the waste bin and started to go through her clothes. Acid-wash jeans and a Red Hot Chili Peppers t-shirt didn't fit the occasion; neither did the plaid baby-doll dress Lily had given her for her sixteenth birthday a week prior. Half of Jade's wardrobe was strewn across her floorboards before she gave up and trudged down the stairs to Margaret's room.

The walls of Margaret's bedroom were pasted with old photographs. Most of them were of people Jade had never met: famous writers and singers whom Margaret idolized enough to tape them directly on her walls. There were a few of Jade, mostly as a baby and toddler, and two of Jade's mother, Caroline.

Jade paused in front of a picture of Caroline going to prom, on the arm of a dark-haired boy with a large mole on one cheek. Caroline was smiling awkwardly, wrapped in light pink taffeta and carrying a small silver purse. Jade had stared at this photograph enough times to know that there were three magnolia trees behind the couple. Caroline had two strands of hair untucked and falling down her cheeks, and the dark-haired boy had six buttons running down the vest of his tuxedo. Jade touched the photograph lightly, wondering where the taffeta dress had ended up. Margaret kept some of Caroline's things in a box in the shed outside;

maybe it was tucked away there.

Rifling through the drawers, Jade found a long black skirt and sweater combination. She wriggled into it in front of her grandmother's mirror, giggling at her reflection. The sweater bagged around her waist, clad in small red beads arranged like flowers. The skirt was loose across her thighs, flowing around her as she twirled in place. This was by no means her style.

"You look lovely," Margaret said from the hallway. She leaned over and tossed her hair around in a towel. "Are you wearing that?"

"I guess so," Jade said, turning around to see how the ensemble looked from behind. "I look like a nun."

Margaret scoffed. "Clearly, you've never seen a nun."

Jade pulled her hair into a high ponytail and secured it with a bright pink scrunchie. "I feel weird going."

"It's the right thing to do," Margaret said simply, as if she had consulted a higher force of morality that morning.

On her way out of the room, Jade spotted the pale seashell on her grandmother's dresser. She remembered sitting on the beach outside their house at six years old, listening to the story of that seashell. Jade had had a bad day up until that point. Someone at school said something to make her upset about her mother. Maybe they'd laughed when she told them Caroline was a treasure hunter. Most kids didn't get it.

"Caroline's in Costa Rica this week," Margaret had explained, trailing her fingers in the loose sand. "Do you know what that is?"

Jade shook her head.

"There are so many mountains, with rainforests at the very top. The trees there… they touch the clouds! And there are monkeys and sloths and flowers that only open at night, when nobody's watching!"

Margaret moved her arms emphatically as she spoke,

as if she were beckoning the rainforest trees to grow out of the beach. Jade imagined great, elephant-foot shaped leaves dripping over them, brilliant emerald snakes slithering out of the sand.

Margaret placed the smooth shell into Jade's small palm. "She found this on the beach and sent it back for you," she whispered. Then she'd turned away from Jade, toward the beach. She'd gone silent, watching the line of sky just above the receding waves.

Jade had looked into the horizon too, trying to see what her grandmother was seeing. She imagined that her mother was rising from under the crashing waves, framed by the slivers of pink and gold fading from the sky, her eyes like polished sea glass and her hands outstretched like sea stars to her mother and daughter.

Chapter Two: A Funeral

The townspeople whispered to each other as they filtered into the pews. It was storming violently outside, so most of them were wearing brightly colored rain coats and boots, which stood out garishly against the black ensembles underneath. Everyone who could make it was there, clutching handkerchiefs that would, in all likelihood, remain dry throughout the ceremony.

None of them had really liked Randy Banks. He was snobbish and peculiar, the townspeople told their spouses as they were getting dressed that morning. He thought he was better than everyone else, just because of his great-great-great grandfather and the college degree that he never put to any real use. Majoring in *maps*! Imagine! But they were all there nonetheless, because, try as they might to belittle him, Randy Banks was the last pillar of the town's legacy, and his death marked the end of an era.

A few of the townspeople were there with more morally questionable motivations. As far as anyone could tell, Randy Banks had no immediate family. He had never married, never fathered children. And, to make matters even more intriguing, there were decades old rumors of a hidden Banks fortune: gold passed down silently through the generations, beginning with Thomas Banks himself. Given the lack of an obvious heir, everyone in town seemed to think they had some chance of receiving Randy's gold.

Margaret guided Jade and Lily into the last pew in the room. They were late, having picked Lily up from her house just minutes before their arrival. Jade had bribed her into coming along by promising her lunch afterward.

"This is weird, Jade," Lily said. "I've seen him maybe twice in my life?"

Jade shrugged. "Remember the sandwiches," she whispered.

A couple of pews down, Lily's stepmother, Linda, was waving furiously at them, her blonde bob moving up and down. Jade waved timidly. She watched as Lily glanced in Linda's direction and then immediately looked away. Linda bit her lip and turned around.

The last people shuffled into their seats and Father John cleared his throat. This was his first time officiating a funeral, and his acne-ridden skin was shining with nervous sweat as he gripped the podium with the white-knuckled insistence of someone clinging to the edge of a cliff. His mother waved at him excitedly from the first row, as if he were a rock star addressing his adoring fans. Father John glared at her and began.

"Brothers and sisters," he said nervously, as if he were asking a question. "We are brought here today to celebrate Randolph Banks, known to friends as 'Randy.' Randolph lived in our town for his entire life. He was an educated man, filled with rich ideas."

Margaret sniffed loudly. Jade turned and saw that her eyes were closed, her lips moving rapidly in prayer. Jade took her grandmother's hand and squeezed it. She wondered whether Margaret and Randy had ever spoken for more than five consecutive minutes. Margaret felt things so strongly that she wouldn't be surprised if they hadn't.

"Randolph's cousin, Eleanor Banks, would like to say a few words now. Miss Banks?" Father John stepped aside as a petite woman stepped up to the podium.

Murmurs filled the room. Linda's voice rung out the loudest. "Banks has a cousin?" she exclaimed.

Eleanor Banks swiped back a strand of hair that had fallen in front of her face. Under the funeral home's glaring light, Jade could make out the large, milky bags under her eyes, and the tightness of her lips: a bow, drawn.

"Randolph," Eleanor said slowly, purposefully. "Was a real character, huh? He sure loved his books, especially those novels."

"Poetry," Margaret whispered beside Jade.

"Well." Eleanor's tone was stiff. She didn't turn to look at the coffin, which Jade thought was odd. She was watching the townspeople. "That's my time, I guess. Have a good afternoon."

"Thank you for that moving tribute, Miss Banks. Now, before we move on to the burial..." Father John said, unfolding a letter in front of him. "A message from Randolph Banks himself, written, we believe, on the day that he passed."

The pews filled with murmuring speculations. Jade wondered whether there was any ice cream left in the freezer at home. She chastised herself for this thought. She hadn't grown up religious, but if there was a God, and he could read her thoughts, he was certainly judging her now.

"I would like to see that note first." Jade looked up to see that Eleanor Banks was speaking. "I should read my cousin's last words first."

Father John cleared his throat uncomfortably, looking around the room as if searching for support. "Well, ma'am, Randolph Banks said he wanted this read to everyone—"

"I'm his blood, aren't I?"

Jade felt a pang of pity for Father John, his hands clasped even tighter around the podium, as though he was afraid Eleanor Banks would take it from him. Jade was very proud of him as he shook his head, let go of the podium, and unfolded the note.

"I really must insist," he said, turning to the paper and

reading the note as quickly as possible. "He said: *Because I could not stop for Death, he kindly stopped for me. The carriage held but just ourselves and immortality.*"

Eleanor Banks started to walk toward Father John, protesting, but Jade wasn't paying attention to her anymore. Randy Banks' words sounded so familiar, like the smell of mulch or the sound of a nursery rhyme: something she'd experienced many times before, but didn't know the name of. She kept repeating the first line in her head as Eleanor Banks stormed out of the funeral home, her lips drawn even tighter than before.

The townspeople recovered quickly from the disruption. They assembled in a line down the middle of the room, taking turns pressing their palms to the polished coffin and returning to their seats with downcast eyes. Jade wondered how many of them had known Randolph Banks. She supposed it didn't matter; death was hard for anyone to see, even if they only experienced the grief second-hand. She wondered if Eleanor Banks was grieving, and that was why she forgot that Randy Banks was known for liking poetry, not novels, and why she didn't stay to put her hand on the coffin.

Margaret and Jade were the last in line. Margaret went first, keeping her distance for a moment, then rushing forward and leaning over the coffin. When she saw his face, she doubled over, sobbing silently and shaking ever so slightly. Jade helped her grandmother back to her seat, making an effort not to look inside the coffin. She'd never seen a dead person before, and she had no desire to.

"Right," Father John said once Jade and Margaret had reached their pew. His voice wavered as he turned to stare at the coffin. "Could I get some help?"

Outside, the rain had subsided but the trees still shook with the wind's intensity. The air smelled of petrichor and sea salt, from the ocean crashing into the shore a block away from them. The procession walked down a short dirt path and into the two-hundred-year-old cemetery, where the coffin was quickly lowered into the damp ground. Father John closed his eyes and said a prayer, and with that, the townspeople dispersed.

"Lily and I were planning on going to Gil's for lunch," Jade said to her grandmother as they walked out of the funeral complex. "But if you want me to come home, I can."

Margaret shook her head. "You two have fun. I'm perfectly fine. Just need a lie-down."

"I'll be back for dinner," Jade said, squeezing her grandmother's forearm and then breaking off in the other direction with Lily.

"Did Randy Banks' note sound familiar to you?" Jade mused as they walked. Lily traversed the edge of the sidewalk like a balance beam, one scuffed-up sneaker in front of the other.

"Nope," Lily said, focused on maintaining her balance. "That was so weird with the cousin."

"Yeah, it was," Jade agreed. "It sounded like a poem. Or part of one, maybe."

"Maybe. Should I get a classic BLT at Gil's, or mix it up and add some avocado?

Jade saw the Paradise Library out of the corner of her eye. She stopped walking. Lily turned around, confused. "What? I know you're not a big fan of avocado, but I like it."

"It is a poem," Jade said. "I must've heard Grandma reciting it."

Lily frowned. "Why do you care where it's from?"

"It's just weird, isn't it? How there are all these rumors, and then he leaves that weird quote out of nowhere, with no context? It's like a clue."

"A clue to..." Lily paused. "Oh." She followed Jade

into the library silently.

Paradise Library was a squat brick building with very little variety to offer. The collection was mostly made up of magazines and cook books, and the town librarian, Ms. Healey was hardly an intellectual. There was a high likelihood of walking in on her with her leg stuck up on the desk, a bottle of nail polish sloshing around in one hand while she painted her big toe with the other. Because of this, the library always smelled vaguely toxic. The smell was especially pungent on this particular day, as Jade swung open the door and Ms. Healey jolted forward, smearing nail polish across her toe.

"Christ on a *stick*," Ms. Healey said, swinging her foot back under her desk and patting her perm. "Jade Adelson, you've gone and given me a heart attack."

"Sorry, Ms. Healey," Jade called as she walked straight to the poetry section. Margaret used to drag her into this corner quite often as a child. Margaret loved reading poetry, memorizing it after a dozen reads or so, and muttering it under her breath to fill the silence. She once told Jade that poetry was the most honest writing in the world. Jade didn't think so; she just found it confusing.

"Will you need help, then?" Ms. Healey called from the corner. One could almost hear her holding her breath, crossing her fingers and newly-painted toes.

"I think we're good, Ms. Healey," Lily replied as Jade pulled a volume off of the shelf.

Ms. Healey exhaled and went back to inspecting her fingernails.

"So, what are we looking for here?" Lily asked dubiously.

"I'm not sure," Jade said as she thumbed through the pages.

"Who's the poet?" When Jade fell silent, Lily groaned and sat down on the green-carpeted floor.

"What's the harm in skimming through, just for a bit?" Jade pleaded. "I promise we'll make it to Gil's."

Lily threw her hands up in defeat and Jade tossed her a hard-back anthology of Robert Frost poems.

"It'll drive me crazy if I don't figure this out," Jade said as she thumbed through a book of Emily Dickinson's poetry.

The library fell into silence as the girls rushed through the pages, save for the sounds of pages falling into each other and Ms. Healey scraping nail polish residue off of her desk. Jade tried to focus on the two lines she knew, but she couldn't help but stop every once in a while to savor the words. She could feel a pulsing lifeline behind the writing, could almost hear the scribble of the poet's pen. She was so immersed in her reading that she read through an entire poem before realizing that it contained what she was searching for.

"I've got it!" Jade exclaimed, holding the open book up like a winning lottery ticket. "Emily Dickinson. 'Because I could not stop for Death.' It's right here!"

Lily clapped her book shut and stood up. Ms. Healey jumped at the sound; she cursed as she screwed up her nail polish again and used her thumb nail to push the bright pink polish off of her big toe. Jade read excitedly, half in a whisper.

Because I could not stop for Death—
He kindly stopped for me—
The Carriage held but just Ourselves—
And Immortality.

Jade trailed off, her eyes narrowing. "Oh, that's rude."

"What is?"

"Someone's *written* in this. My grandma would flip if she saw this."

Lily leaned over Jade's shoulder to see. On the corner of the page, a series of numbers was written in wavering blue ink.

43.7844° N, 88.7879° W
38.9108° N, 75.5277° W
32.3182° N, 86.9023° W

"They're coordinates," Lily said, taking the book and looking at it intently. "Right?"

"Coordinates," Jade said. "Like, X-marks-the-spot?"

"Oh boy," Lily said. "Please don't go down this road."

"Maybe," Jade said quickly. "Randy Banks left us a clue. Maybe this is where his gold is hidden."

"That rumor doesn't make any sense. If Randy Banks had gold, he wouldn't have lived here."

"It's his family home! Come on, this is just like the treasure hunts we used to do."

"Exactly," Lily said.

Jade had spent many afternoons of their friendship pulling Lily through the swamps on the other side of town, insisting that she knew of treasure buried deep below them. They would dig and dig and dig, imagining rubies the size of grapefruits and bars of gold dusted in dirt, only to find a clump of worms, or a web of roots. Jade saw clues everywhere. She imagined herself walking behind her mother, following in her gold-stained tracks.

Jade's treasure-hunting fervor died down once they reached high school. One night, when the two girls were having a sleepover in Jade's attic room, she turned over in the bed and said to Lily, out of nowhere, "I don't think she's coming back." At sixteen years old, it seemed that her childhood was gone, and even if Caroline came home now, it was too late. There was a gap between them that Jade wouldn't know how to fill. Lily had nodded understandingly, not asking who wasn't coming back or how Jade felt about that.

Now, though, Lily looked baffled. "Jade," she said slowly. "There's no gold."

"This makes *sense*," Jade said, hugging the book against her chest. "I mean, why else would there be coordinates in the book?"

"Jade," Lily said slowly. "Remember the story you told me about Mr. Werner's petunias?"

On an early summer morning in 1986, Jade's neighbor, Mr. Werner, had awoken to the sound of a seven-year old Jade Adelson ripping the petunias out of the garden bed in his front yard. When asked later by her grandmother, Jade explained that Mr. Werner had hidden his wife's jewelry under the flowers.

"Oh, come on," Jade laughed. "That was stupid, okay? But this— this is *real*."

"I really think we should let this go."

"Come on, we'll just get a map, check what the coordinates—"

"Jade," Lily said bluntly. "This isn't going to help."

"Help what?"

Lily looked down at her Converses while she spoke. The edges were peeling up, the Sharpie-drawn smiley faces looked up at her encouragingly. "These hunts," she said, still watching her shoes. "They only disappoint you."

"This isn't about her," Jade said quickly. "I swear, it isn't."

"Are you s—"

"It's not!" Jade exclaimed, her voice growing louder than she'd anticipated. "Jesus, Lily, leave me alone!"

Lily bit the side of her mouth, so her cheek sucked inward a little. "You're doing the thing, Jade."

"What thing?"

"You're steamrolling me."

Jade took a deep breath. "I'm sorry. I don't mean to steamroll. I just— this doesn't seem weird to you? The cousin, the poem, these coordinates? It feels like it's all stacking up to something bigger." She paused, and when Lily said nothing, she continued. "Can we just pull up a map, look at the coordinates. If they mean nothing, we give this up."

Lily nodded reluctantly. "Okay."

Jade walked around the bookshelf to see Ms. Healey brushing bright blue eye shadow across her eyelids. "Do you have a world map here by any chance?"

Ms. Healey gestured toward the other corner of the room, where all science-related books had been thrown into lopsided piles. Jade opened an atlas and trace along the latitude and longitude lines, imagining the map coming alive: the blue-stained oceans tossing, clashing, becoming real, the crunches of mountains rising out of the one-dimensional. Her two chipped-pink nails converged over the state of Wisconsin. The second time, Delaware, and the third, Alabama. Jade's hands fell to her sides.

"Wisconsin, Delaware, Alabama," she muttered. She turned to Lily, who had been watching the map from over her shoulder. "That mean anything?"

Lily shook her head. "I'm sorry, Jade, I don't think it does."

Jade looked at the map for a few more moments, as if some hint might reveal itself if intimidated into doing so. She sighed. "It's fine. Let's just go."

Ms. Healey was applying mascara as the girls walked past her desk. She lowered the wand and blinked, leaving stripes of black along her under-eyes. "Are you taking that with you? You'll need to check it out," she said, looking pointedly at the Emily Dickinson poetry volume that Lily had forgotten to put down.

"Oh," Lily said. "No, I'll go put it back."

Ms. Healey squinted as Lily passed her with the book. "Weird," she mumbled. "Some lady was *just* in here with that book. Asked if she could take it, but she didn't have a library card."

"Who was she?" Jade asked abruptly. Few people in Paradise were known to spend their summer days at the library, much less in the poetry section.

"Don't know, do I? That's why I wouldn't give it to her." Ms. Healey looked up and saw that they were watching her and listening to her with the same intensity she gave to gossip magazines. She leaned forward, lowered her voice. "And then she wrote something down on her hand and just *left*! Isn't that strange?"

Chapter Three: Wisconsin, Delaware, and Alabama

There were three restaurants and four bars in Paradise, North Carolina, all of which were lined up against each other on Main Street. Two of the restaurants served only seafood, which made Lily feel sick, so she and Jade always went to the third option, *Gil's Sandwiches and Bagels*. The shop owner, Gil, was a stringy old man with a full head of gray hair that jutted upwards as if immune to the effects of gravity or balding.

"You know, I'm going to be honest with you ladies. I've had a hell of a week." Gil asked as he set their sandwiches down in front of them.

When Jade had first met Gil, she'd been taken aback. His earnestness was so genuine that it felt fake, like every word he spoke was playing a joke on himself. Even now, he smiled while he spoke, opening up to two teenage girls as if they were his best friends.

"Sorry to hear that, Gil," Lily said, raising the BLT to her mouth. She'd opted for no avocado. "Could I have some mayo?"

Gil continued to speak as he went into the kitchen, but they could hardly hear him."It's hard, you know. Running a business in a town like this," he yelled from behind the swinging kitchen door. "The economy…" His voice was cut off by the sounds of plastic bottles falling from the cupboards, bouncing against the linoleum flooring. A few seconds later, he reemerged with a bottle of mayonnaise, handing it to Lily with an air of defeat.

"Thanks," Lily said, straining to conceal a smirk. "I didn't know there was anything wrong with the economy." She squirted a long line of mayonnaise across one slice of bread and pressed it against the rest of the sandwich.

"Well, neither did I," Gil said. "But then I heard about your dad. How's he doing, by the way?"

Lily's face went stony as she lowered her sandwich back to the plate, seconds before she could take a bite. "What? What's wrong with Al?"

Lily was the only person Jade knew who called her father by his first name. But, then again, Lily was the only person in town whose father owned a bar and had been arrested for selling counterfeit purses. The first time Jade met Al, it was Lily's fourth birthday party. Everyone from Paradise Elementary School was invited, but few showed up. Al walked in late, just as they were cutting the cake. Linda was with him; Jade remembered wondering if she was Lily's sister, and being astonished when she later discovered her to be Al's girlfriend. Lily's mother let them in but glared at them the whole time. Al skulked in the corner, eating his slice of ice cream cake so intently that the blue icing smeared across his bright red beard. His beard was a subject of unprecedented gossip in Paradise. His head was smooth and bald, but that beard remained the invigorated red of a much younger man. Many of the bar's visitors were there, at least in part, to wager their bets on whether the beard was real or dyed.

"Erm," Gil was twisting around in his seat uncomfortably. "I'm sorry, I thought you'd know." He looked to Jade for support, but she wasn't sure what to say. "The bar's shutting down— I just heard."

Lily was frowning down at her sandwich. Jade remembered two months ago, when Lily's mom got laid off from her job at the grocery store. She knew that Al was still paying child support; Lily made jokes about having to be nice to him because of it. How much were they relying on it?

Lily wiped mayonnaise and bacon juice off of her chin with a paper napkin. "I'm sorry, Jade," she said. "I need to go talk to Mom."

"Of course." Jade's chair screeched as she stood up, pushing it back with the insides of her knees. "I'll walk you home."

Lily shook her head. "Have to clear my head," she said simply. "Talk later?"

Jade nodded and sat back down. Lily grabbed the sandwich off her plate, reached into her pocket, and handed Gil a five-dollar bill.

"Oh, no," Gil insisted, offering it back to her. "Keep it."

Lily frowned at him. For a moment, Jade worried that she might explode on him. But she pushed her chair in and walked out, the glass door swinging creakily behind her.

"I didn't know," Gil said as they watched her leave, rounding the corner of Main Street and disappearing from view.

"She'll be fine," Jade said after a moment. "They'll be fine."

"I saw you were at the funeral," Gil said. Jade turned to him and saw that he was biting his lip, his eyes staring passively ahead. "Did you know Randy well?"

"No," Jade said. "My grandma did. I just knew *of* him."

"Hmph," Gil responded, his voice tired. "Sadly, I think that's all most people in this town can say."

Chapter Four: Sonata

Margaret was sitting in the living room with her eyes closed when Jade got home. An old opera record was playing, and the timbres of the singers' voices mixed with the sounds of the wind chimes outside to create an otherworldly effect. The singer's pleas were getting more urgent, mounting exponentially in intensity. He was screaming in Italian, and even though Margaret didn't speak any language other than English, she was swinging along, her eyes squeezed shut and her hands clamped around the chair arms.

"Grandma," Jade asked.

Margaret raised her eyebrows and then slowly opened her eyes. "You were with Lily?" she asked. There was an odd quality to the way in which Margaret posed questions. Something about the inflections she used made them sound more like demands.

"Yeah. We went and saw Gil."

"Odd man," Margaret said. The opera singer exploded with emotion and she closed her eyes again. Jade sat down on the couch.

"Did you hear about Wide Al's?"

"Lily's dad's bar?" Margaret kept her eyes closed as she spoke.

"Yeah," Jade said. "It's going out of business."

"Hm," Margaret said, opening one eye skeptically. "Well, it is empty all the time, isn't it? And Mr. Treen is such a vulgar man. Covered with tattoos. You won't get a tattoo, will you?"

Conversations with Margaret always went this way. Jade would offer up a subject, and then Margaret would twist around it, skipping from one idea to the next. Jade had learned to dismiss the last thing her grandmother said each time she talked, as it rarely related to the matter at hand.

"No," Jade said. "I'm just worried. About Lily."

Margaret reached over and took Jade's hands. The inlaid stone on her ring scratched at Jade's skin. "I'm sorry, darling," she said sadly. "I'm sure she'll be fine. It all works out in the end."

Jade could deduce quite a bit from the way Margaret spoke. When she spouted out platitudes, as she was today, she was distant, bothered. Margaret stood up, pulled her long denim skirt down, and walked over to the record player. Jade cringed as she turned the dial and the opera singer roared tempestuously.

"I'm going to my room," Jade said, moving as quickly as she could away from the screaming record player.

The music followed her up the two flights of stairs and into her room. She imagined the sound crawling through the cracks in the floorboards, rebounding off of the walls and concentrating itself in the corners of her room. Her bedroom was the only uncluttered room in the house. There were no photographs pasted to the walls, no watercolor paintings or poetry books with a few pages torn out. She had a king-sized bed with an old mahogany headboard and a navy-blue bedspread, a chest of drawers overflowing with clothes she'd grown out of long ago, and a desk with one photograph on it: her and her grandmother, faces painted and smiling, at the Paradise Zoo.

Deep in the drawer of Jade's desk, covered with a stapler, a hole puncher, and a stack of papers, was a stack of letters Jade had written, but never sent, to Caroline. They dated back to when she was six years old and could hardly write, yet needed a place to voice her frustrations. The paper was worn with time and re-reading. Most of them had been around when Jade was in middle school, back when she liked to tuck them under her pillow while she slept. She would imagine that, by sleeping with her thoughts so close to her, she could somehow enter her mother's dreams. She had plenty of theories like that.

Now that she was alone in her room again, Margaret's music drowning out even the comforting sounds of the wind chimes outside, Jade found herself staring at the drawer, driven from habit to write down what she was feeling. She allowed herself to reimagine her childhood fantasy one more time. She saw, in her mind's eye, a scribbled, desperate apology, a letter, this time written by Caroline instead of Jade, an assurance that she was on her way back, that she wanted to change.

As a child, Jade hadn't cried much. She never kicked or bit people, never used "potty-words," as her kindergarten teacher called them. But as she sat in her room on this particular day, she wanted to kick and bite and curse. She could feel something tilting inside of her. The funeral, the failed treasure hunt, Wide Al's, the letter in her desk, Wisconsin, Delaware, Alabama. Wisconsin, Delaware, Alabama. Wisconsin, Delaware, Al— Jade froze. Was she crazy, she wondered as she sat there, questioning her realization. Was Lily right? Was she projecting all of her stress onto this small, uncontrollable thing?

But it couldn't be a coincidence. Jade ran down to the kitchen and picked up the phone by its chunky sky-blue handle. Lily picked up after four suspenseful rings.

"Hello?"

"Lily! It's Jade. I think I figured it out." Jade said, twirling the phone cord between her knuckles.

"Figured what…" Lily trailed off. "Jade, I'm sorry, but I can't do this right now."

"Wisconsin, Delaware, Alabama," Jade said, cutting off a long sigh from Lily. "Think about that, Lily. Think about the abbreviations. W-I, D-E, A-L."

There was a moment of silence.

"Lily?" Jade asked. "You still there?"

"Mom needs me tonight," Lily said hesitantly. "I'll be there tomorrow morning."

Chapter Five: Wide Al's

"Do you want to talk about—" Jade cut herself off. She stopped pumping her feet as she veered her bicycle onto the sidewalk.

"No," Lily said, raising her voice over the chugging sounds of a passing truck. She followed Jade, groaning as she rolled over a hole in the pavement.

The sun had only just reached the top rung of clouds in the sky as they turned onto Main Street. Few people were out at that hour. There were the shopkeepers, slouched over their cash registers like zombies, and the occasional restless retiree taking a morning walk, pumping their one-pound weights in front of them. But for the most part, Paradise on a weekend morning was as desolate as the ocean itself, with those awake passing each other silently like sail boats following the wind.

When they reached Wide Al's, leaning their bikes up against the store front, Lily pushed the door open without knocking. As usual, the bar was empty. Jade supposed it would be more depressing to see people there in the morning than to see no one there at all. Al was sitting on the customers' side of the bar, talking on the phone. The cord was wrapped around his hand, like he was scared the phone would fall if there was nothing keeping it up but his clammy-handed grip.

"That's what I said!" Al said, laughing wholeheartedly. He turned and saw Lily and Jade. "Listen, man, I gotta go. See you at the party tonight?"

The person on the other end of the line said something, and Al chuckled to himself as he hung up. He stopped smiling when he saw Lily's face.

"Did you get Mom's calls?" She asked, crossing her arms.

Al scratched his head. "Lil', I'm not talking to that woman for a million bucks," he said. "I know she's your mom, but she's a real—"

"Never mind," Lily said, cutting him off. "Just tell me what you'll do now."

"Eat lunch," Al responded gruffly. "That alright with you?"

"Stop joking, Al. Will you get a new job?"

"Why would I do that?"

"Because you're broke."

Al started to laugh. Lily's face reddened.

"It's not funny! How are you going to live? Mom's still trying to find a job, and you—"

"I told you, Lil-bug, I don't want to talk about your mom. Just listen to me, alright?"

"Don't call me that. And you're going to a *party* tonight?"

Jade looked around for an escape. Maybe she could go to the bathroom while they talked? She wrinkled her nose at the thought; she had gone into that bathroom once before, and the smell trickled back into her memory uninvitingly.

"I don't know what I expected," Lily said incisively. "You're a drunk."

"A drunk," Al repeated, his hands drumming against the bar surface.

"A drunk," Lily said again.

"You… you know, you're just like her!" Al said. He started to stumble on his words. "You don't visit for… how long? Months, it feels like. And now you're here to insult me and get my money."

"What money?" Lily said sarcastically.

"You'd be surprised," Al said. He smiled smugly.

Lily rolled her eyes.

"I'm serious," Al said. He sounded like a young child pleading with a parent, waiting for them to pay attention and believe him.

"Then why's the bar going under?" Lily asked abrasively.

"Bar going under? Who've you been talking to?"

"Gil said—"

"Gil? Old man's got no idea what he's talking about."

"So you aren't losing this place?"

"Losing it?" Al laughed again. "I'm selling it! And for more than a pretty penny, I'll tell you that much."

"No one wants this dump," Lily said dryly.

"Tell that to…" Al trailed off, scratched the red stubble on his neck. He got up and fetched a wad of papers from the other end of the bar. He squinted down at the print. "Eleanor, that's her name. Eleanor Banks."

"Banks?" Jade asked. "Like Randy Banks?"

"His cousin," Al said. "Walked in here yesterday and said she'd pay twice what this place is worth."

"What's she going to do with it?" Lily said, scanning the bare, pungent room skeptically.

"Who knows?" Al said. "But she said this place was gold. *Gold*." He laughed, slapping his knee for effect.

Lily and Jade let the words sink in. They turned to each other, their eyes meeting just as they reached the same conclusion.

"Bet you feel bad now!" Al said smugly, oblivious to their locked gaze. "Getting mad at your old man like that!"

"When're you moving out?" Lily said, still looking at Jade.

"Day after tomorrow," Al said. "Hey, you could make all this up to me by helping me pack."

Lily frowned and opened her mouth to tell him off, but Jade grabbed her wrist and squeezed it.

"Of course, Mr. Treen," Jade said appreciatively. "We would love to help."

Al smiled appreciatively, revealing a set of yellow-tinted teeth. Lily glared at Jade as he waved them over to the backroom. They stopped at the threshold, frozen in awe.

"Dad, you've got to be kidding me," Lily said scathingly. "When was the last time you cleaned?"

Al leaned against a slanted column of cardboard boxes and shrugged. Around him, overfilled boxes of empty liquor bottles, paperwork, and god-knows-what-else were stacked on top of each other like great, molding building blocks. "It got a bit out of hand," Al admitted as he fanned a fly off of his cheek. "I couldn't ask him to clean it up, though, could I, what with him being sick."

"Him?"

"Randy Banks," Al said. "Rest his soul."

"This is his stuff?"

"He rented the room out a couple months back. Said he needed the extra storage. I thought it'd just be a couple boxes, you know, and I needed the extra money." Al gave Lily an evil eye. "Not that I need it anymore."

"Did you tell Randy's cousin about his things being here?"

"You think I'm a real idiot, don't you? I wasn't about to tell her about this mess and make her bring down her price. No, I said the whole place was clean as a whistle. We need to get rid of all of this before she gets here."

"We?" Lily asked, scanning the room with disgust.

"We'll help," Jade said quickly.

"I'll give you some allowance, Lil-bug," Al offered. "Ice cream money, like when you were little."

Lily rolled her eyes as he left the room. "This is shaping up to be as bad of a day as yesterday," she muttered bitterly as she lifted a cardboard box from the top of a stack.

The bottom of the box gave out and a stack of books fell to the ground, splaying across the concrete. One of them fell on Lily's foot; she hopped around, cursing lightly while Jade bent over and picked the books up.

"Poetry!" Jade exclaimed. "He had poetry books."

"My mom has poetry books," Lily said grumpily. "That doesn't mean she reads them. And she definitely doesn't have any gold."

Jade gave her an unappreciative frown. "Guess what's on the top of the pile," she asked smugly.

"How to Hide a Million Dollars in Gold?" Lily muttered, moving on to another box.

"Emily Dickinson."

The next few boxes yielded less interesting results. They shuffled through tax returns, prescriptions, grocery store lists. It seemed that Randy Banks had not disposed of anything, nor had he organized it in any way. His birth certificate was sandwiched between a Bojangles receipt and a picture of him as a baby, sitting in the grass wearing only a diaper.

"This is depressing," Lily said as she pulled a coffee-stained map out of the pile and spread it out. "This stuff belongs in the dump."

"Don't be mean, Lily." Jade suddenly felt defensive of Randy Banks. Surely, there was more to his life than what could be contained in these cardboard boxes. Had he ever loved anyone, ever walked along the beach and wondered whether there were dolphins or sharks underneath the still currents? She wondered how many boxes she could fill with her own life. Maybe two, at most, and the majority of the space would be taken up by letters she had never sent.

Her grandmother, on the other hand, would take up a whole warehouse full of boxes. The wind chimes alone would take up a fair amount of room, along with the poetry anthologies, the framed bird paintings, the newspaper clippings and records and dangling shell earrings. Jade chastised herself for thinking about death so objectively.

Her mother's boxes wouldn't contain a trace of her. They would be filled with artifacts and archaeological dissertations, not birth certificates and baby blankets. Did Caroline still have Jade's birth certificate, or had she given that to Margaret as well?

"Jade, come look at this," Lily said. She had surrounded herself with unfolded maps, so that they formed a circle around her feet.

Jade walked over and looked at each of the maps, but she couldn't see anything unusual. They all depicted the town of Paradise. Major landmarks were pinpointed: Wide Al's, the Banks family estate, the Paradise Library, the fishing pier. Jade could even see where her house was, just along the coast.

"What about it?" she asked, confused.

"There's always something missing," Lily said excitedly.

Jade looked at Lily and remembered the first treasure hunt she'd dragged them on, not long after they became friends. She'd heard a rumor from Ms. Healey while visiting the library with Margaret: someone had found a gold necklace buried in the sand on the beach, but the stone that was once inside of it was missing. Jade had searched through Margaret's shed until she found an old metal detector. She and Lily took turns sweeping the beach near her house. The first twenty times the metal detector went off, Lily's face lit up. She was making the same face now that she had when she dug through the sand back then, her eyes pinched up and her cheeks flushed with excitement.

"Missing?" Jade prompted her.

Lily pointed at the map directly in front of her. "See, I was looking at this one, and I noticed that Wide Al's was missing from the map." Lily turned to the next map. "And this one. There's Wide Al's, but no library."

Lily was right. There were blank spaces in the places where major town institutions should have been.

"Here," Lily continued, picking up the next map. "Why wouldn't he include his own house?"

Jade nodded, her mind whirring. She scanned the other maps. They continued to omit key pieces of the town.

"The only constant..." Lily prodded, clearly satisfied with herself.

"The fishing pier."

"Dad!" Lily yelled out. "We're leaving."

Chapter Six: The Pier

Half of the fishing pier had splintered into the sea in the great hurricane of 1854, and no one had bothered to reconstruct it. Instead, the town council did a hasty job of boarding up the end of the pier, so that it stopped just where the water started at low tide. It didn't go far out enough for any proper fishing, and the rickety structure creaked alarmingly with strong gusts of wind, so few ever ventured far out on it.

Paradise's middle schoolers used to dare each other to run down to the end of the pier, push off of the makeshift edge, and run back, gritting their teeth and praying that they didn't collapse into the water in a flowering crash of waves and wooden boards. A few years back, one boy swore the pier swayed under him while he was running, and his friends insisted he was telling the truth. Since then, the game had lost its popularity, and the pier had remained unused, weighed down with pounds of barnacles and creeping sea grass.

As usual, today, the pier was empty. And as a result of the looming gray clouds, the beach itself was empty as Jade and Lily walked down to the pier. The waves were streaked with green, frothing from the wind's lashes. Jade could easily imagine the entire pier being uprooted from the ocean floor and knocked onto the sand.

"Do you think he could've buried it under the pier?" she asked Lily.

"Let's hope so," Lily said, crossing her fingers. "I am

not going on that thing."

The tide was low, so they walked back and forth under the pier's cracking belly. They lifted every oddly colored shell, dug shallow holes around the pier's legs. There was nothing to suggest the presence of buried treasure. Jade suddenly feared that Randy Banks hadn't accounted for his gold being pulled away by the winds and water.

"Maybe we could try—"

"Jade," Lily said, interrupting her friend mid-thought. "If you suggest that we dig around this whole area, so help me."

"Just a thought," Jade said, throwing her hands up. "Maybe a metal detector?"

"Oh, yeah, let me just whip out my portable metal detector that I bring everywhere," Lily said. "Come on, who do we know that has a metal detector?"

Jade looked at Lily knowingly.

"Ah," Lily said, immediately understanding. "Right."

Margaret's house was just a couple of blocks from the pier, so they reached it within a matter of minutes. Jade kicked a piece of loose gravel across the better part of the distance.

"What does she use it for?" Lily asked as Jade overshot and the piece of gravel landed in a neighbor's lawn.

"I don't know," Jade said, propelling the rock forward against the sidewalk. "I've never actually seen her use it. It kind of just sits in the shed."

"Do you think it's your mom's?"

"Maybe. Yeah, that'd make sense."

They found Margaret sitting on the back porch, surrounded by her wind chimes. Jade strained to hear music coming from inside but didn't hear any, indicating that Margaret might be feeling better than she had the day before.

"Grandma?" Jade yelled out as they approached the

house.

Margaret turned to her as if torn from a very important thought. Jade recognized her gaze: the slack jaw, the wide, confused eyes. This was the same expression she wore whenever she talked about Caroline.

"What's wrong?" Jade asked as she drew closer.

"With me?" Margaret asked coyly. "Oh, nothing. Just watching the ocean. Are you going swimming today?"

Jade looked around the beach: the tempestuous winds, the jagged waves slapping against the sand. "It's not exactly the right weather," she said. "We're using the metal detector, okay?"

"Metal detector?" Margaret frowned. "What on Earth for?"

"Just playing around on the beach."

Margaret started to open her mouth, but then she closed it, nodded, and turned back to the ocean. As Jade walked away with Lily, towards the shed, she felt worry blooming inside of her, its thorns poking at the insides of her ribs. The normal Margaret wouldn't have settled for such a simple response; she would've poked and prodded and, finally, joined Jade and Lily on their adventure. Jade wondered if Margaret was finally getting old. She wasn't like most grandmothers; she still dyed and cropped her hair into an auburn red bob and she preferred brisk morning swims to knitting and crochet. Maybe Margaret was just shaken up by Randy's funeral, but Jade couldn't see why she took it so personally.

Jade swung open the shed door, bursting a series of tightly-strung cobwebs. The shed was cluttered with just about everything that didn't fit in the house. In a way, Jade realized, the shed was Margaret's version of a room full of boxes. She found the metal detector tucked behind a trash bag filled with her childhood toys.

It was heavier than she had expected. Based on the rust

growing like thin vines along its sides, Margaret must have gotten it a long time ago. Jade hoisted it up with both hands and carried it out to where Lily was waiting, bunching her sleeves in her fists. Lily took one end of the appliance and they lugged it back to the pier, Jade carrying a large-faced shovel in her other hand. Margaret had used it for gardening, back when she gardened. This phase had lasted for around half a year, until a single plant wilted and died. That day, Margaret dug up all of her remaining plants, gave them to the next door neighbor, and vowed never to garden again.

Jade and Lily passed a couple of walking groups on their way: clusters of retirees who couldn't afford Florida, wearing bright purple exercise vests and sneakers with medically prescribed insoles. They glanced at the girls as they stormed by.

When Jade and Lily reached the beach, they lowered the metal detector onto the sand.

"I have a new appreciation for treasure hunters," Lily said. "Your mom must be super buff."

Jade laughed, imagining her mother, sparkles on her face, arms arched upwards like the famous wrestlers she saw on magazine covers. "We need to make sure we cover everything," she said as she scanned the area under the pier. "I'll start over at the end here, and then you can take over when my arm starts falling off?"

She moved across the damp sand methodically, walking in straight lines and then looping back in the other direction like a farmer plowing a field. After only a few strides, the metal detector emitted a sharp, piercing noise. Lily scrambled for the shovel excitedly and started to dig erratically, sand catching in the wind as it flew from the shovel's mouth.

"Do you know how deep we'll have to dig?" she asked, dumping another clump of sand next to the widening hole.

Before Jade could respond, Lily plunged the shovel back into the sand and hit something solid. She bent down and parted the sand with her hands. Something shiny glowed up at them; as Jade realized what it was, she wondered if it was taunting them.

"A soda can," Lily said disappointedly. She put the can to the side and refilled the hole. When Jade passed the metal detector over the section of sand again, it fell silent.

"It's okay," Jade said, mostly to herself. "It wouldn't have been a treasure hunt if we found it that quickly." She went back to scanning the land. She imagined that her mother was watching her, peering through the cracks in the pier boards to see her only daughter, doing exactly what she had done at that age.

"Once, my mom was in Italy, and some other treasure hunter was looking for the same necklace she was looking for," Jade said, remembering one her favorite childhood bedtime stories. "So she went to a local jeweler and bought a fake. And then once she'd found the necklace, in the wall of a noble family's mansion, she put the fake in there. Apparently, her rival found the fake and didn't notice the difference. He brought it to his boss, a rich collector, and he—"

The metal detector went haywire, screaming in an even higher pitch than before. Jade quickly moved it away, and Lily started to dig. A single scoop revealed a weathered dime, clotted over with wet sand.

"It says 1906!" Lily said, scraping the sand off. "That's kind of cool."

Jade nodded, but she could feel her disappointment deepening. She kept going, sweeping the detector across the sand.

"What happened to the rival?" Lily asked.

Jade thought about this for a moment. "I'm not sure, actually. Probably got fired or something."

Over the course of the next hour, they found three bottle caps, a loose piece of wire, and a silver ring corroded with rust. Lily was happy enough every time they found something, but Jade found it hard to keep going. Her arm was growing weaker and her head was starting to pulse with a headache. A slight drizzle started to fall around them, slanting with the wind so that it reached below the pier.

Lily took over once Jade had covered half of the area. Jade sat down in the sand and looked out at the ocean, which had been creeping toward them silently as time wore on. She felt exactly as she had at seven years old, standing in front of a gaping hole in Mr. Werner's garden, trying to explain why his petunias had been torn up and tossed around the garden. He'd walked her back to Margaret, who had apologized profusely and promised she would give Jade a stern talking to. Instead, she'd given Jade a bowl of ice cream, sat her down, and watched the clock in silence for several moments. Then she had apologized to Jade.

"Jade, honey," she'd said. Jade could tell, even at that age, that her grandmother was grasping at her words, turning them around in her mouth and trying to decide if they were right. "I know I've told you lots of stories about treasure hunting, and I know you look up to your Mom for doing it."

Margaret paused and Jade nodded in agreement as she ate another mouthful of chocolate ice cream. It smeared across her lips, and Margaret leaned over to clean her cheeks with a napkin.

"But we have to be careful," she continued. "Not everyone thinks like us. Some people just want to have their flowers, instead of digging to see what's under them."

She'd sent Jade back with a store-bought bouquet of flowers, which now struck Jade as rather ironic. Jade had given them to Mr. Werner and apologized for digging into his nice flowers, even though she remained convinced that there were jewels hidden somewhere in his backyard. She still eyed his new prized rosebush every time she passed it on the way to school, but, for her grandmother's sake, she didn't dig.

"Jade!" Lily said. She'd called her name twice now, yelling over the noises of the activated metal detector. "We've got another one."

Jade pushed herself up, grabbed the shovel, and started to dig. Before long, she hit another disappointing soda can, buried against the side of one of the pier's posts. She went to toss it into the pile, but Lily stopped her.

"What's that sticking out of it?" Lily asked, reaching out to take the soda can.

Jade reached her fingers into the lip of the can and pulled out a small, tightly rolled slip of paper. She unfurled it quickly, grains of sand falling to the ground in a heavy cloud as she shook it off and read it.

Go back to the place where it all began. I love you, and I'm so glad I met you. -R.B.

Lily and Jade exchanged a scandalized glance.

"Who do you think he's talking to?" Lily asked after a moment. "He wouldn't tell his cousin he was glad to meet her, right?"

"It sounds like Randy Banks had a girlfriend," Jade said, raising her eyebrows. "And she was supposed to find his treasure."

"Should we stop, then?"

Jade and Lily looked down at the note. The handwriting was frantic, erratic, genuine. Randy Banks had loved someone, and as the sun flashed through the curtain of falling mist, it seemed only right that it was that someone who found his treasure. Lily rolled the slip back up wordlessly and pushed it back into the can. She dropped it with a slight thud, and Jade packed the sand back on top of it. They looked at the mound for a few moments.

"It's the right thing to do," Lily said, placing her hand on Jade's shoulder.

"I know. It's just disappointing."

They scooped up their assorted collection of junk, the metal detector, and the shovel, and started back towards the house. The rain had subsided for some time, and the air felt pure in a way it hadn't in a couple of days. Jade imagined that she was breathing out for the first time in two days: breathing out her mission, her commitment to the treasure hunt. The place where it all began, she thought to herself. Where would that be? Where the treasure hunt began, or maybe where the lovers met? Or at the Banks house, where his life itself began? She pushed down her desire to run to every possible location.

When they reached the house, they found Margaret listening to opera music again. As soon as Lily heard it, she insisted that it was time she went home. They deposited their worthless loot in the garbage can and said their goodbyes, and then Jade walked inside. Margaret was rearranging a row of shells on the windowsill. They had previously been ordered by size, but now she was arranging them by color.

"Grandma?" Jade asked, shutting the door behind her softly so as to avoid startling her.

Margaret turned to her, smiling softly. "Your mother and I used to travel all the time," she said, and Jade could tell that there was a story coming. Margaret scooped up the shells, laid them out on the middle cushion of the couch, and sat down on one end. Jade joined her on the other end. She traced their edges as she spoke. "All kinds of places, all over the East Coast, but mostly to beaches. Your mother loved the beach. She was so..." Margaret frowned. "Fearless."

Margaret picked up a spike-rimmed conch shell and looked at it as if it were telling her a story. She put it down suddenly and looked back up at Jade.

"She would jump right into the waves, just like you did when you were little. Do you remember?"

Jade nodded.

"Do you remember how scared I was?"

Jade remembered salt water in her nose and eyes, hair slopped over her face and sand in her bathing suit as Margaret scooped her up by the armpits.

"I hated the beach then," Margaret admitted. "It always seemed so violent to me. Like its mission was to push everyone over. Like a bully."

"Yeah," Jade said slowly.

"But she just loved it. She would roll with them, see, just lift her feet up and let them sweep her down. She always got up again, no matter how hard the waves hit." Margaret frowned. "There was once, though, she didn't get up. Not for a really long time. And I thought—" Her voice caught on the words and she reached for Jade's hand. "I was so angry at her for putting herself in danger like that."

Jade nodded, even though the story didn't make much sense to her.

Margaret smiled appreciatively. "So you understand? Why I was angry? You don't blame me?"

"Grandma," Jade said softly, putting her hand on top of her grandmother's. "You're not making any sense."

"I'm sorry," Margaret said, nodding sadly. Her skin was translucent in the evening night. For a moment, Jade imagined that Margaret was kneeling on the shadowed floor of the ocean, sending nothing but air bubbles up to Jade, who was floating face-down, trying to understand what she was saying.

Chapter Seven: Eleanor Banks' Visit

The next morning, Jade woke up to Margaret making breakfast. This was rare; the average breakfast in their house was a bowl of stale Count Chocula swimming in chocolate milk. Margaret once admitted to Jade that she didn't like cereal much— she just loved the little trinkets stored inside the boxes. She kept all of them in a big cardboard box in the shed: brittle superhero figurines, plastic whistles, even a small pinball game.

So when Jade woke up the smell of bacon for the first time in years, she wondered if the house was on fire. She half-ran, half-walked down the stairs and into the kitchen, only to find Margaret wrapped up in a turquoise cotton robe, her feet tucked into bright pink bunny slippers that Jade had given her for her last birthday. She was flipping a misshapen pancake, the edges seared with burnt butter. Jade noted that there was jazz music playing.

"Chocolate chips or blueberries?" Margaret asked.

Jade slid into her chair. "Blueberry, please." She paused. Margaret's birthday was in November—she was sure of that. "Is there a special occasion I'm missing?"

"No, no. Oh! Lily called," Margaret added as she plopped a pancake on a plate and added a swirling cone of whipped cream. "She seemed pretty rattled—I would call back quickly."

Jade nodded. She went to the living room and slid her fingers into the coiling rings of the phone cord as she typed Lily's number in. She'd memorized it back in the second grade, after she accidentally called 9-1-1 because, as she had insisted to a very upset Margaret, "it sounded familiar."

The line rang twice before Lily picked it up.

"Jade!" she said quickly. "That you?"

"Yup."

"We have a problem."

"Ask if she wants pancakes!" Margaret yelled.

Lily's house was only a five minute bike ride away, so she arrived quickly. She shoveled down a blueberry pancake to appease Margaret, who was wearing her apron as an athlete might wear an Olympic medal, and then gestured towards the stairs leading to Jade's room.

"Grandma, we're gonna go talk super quickly," Jade said. "Back in a jiff!"

Lily shut the door behind them and then turned to Jade, pressing her hands against her cheeks in almost comical distress.

"What?" Jade sat down on her bed. "This had better be the end of the world, the way you're acting."

"I was just with my dad for breakfast," Lily said quickly. "He made the worst scrambled eggs of my life," she added. "But that's not the point. He was bragging about the sale, and he said Eleanor Banks, you know, Randy's cousin, was coming over *today*. To see the place."

She waited for Jade to react for a moment, and then had another burst of excitement. "So let's go!"

"Go where?" Jade sat down on the end of her bed. She wondered: if she fell asleep right then and there, could she wake up only for dinner, and then fall back asleep again?

"My dad's bar!" Lily said. "We have to get the maps before she sees them."

"What are you talking about?"

Lily sighed and sat down next to Jade. "If Randy Banks' cousin sees those maps, it'll probably take her a minute or two, but she'll figure it out just like we did."

"And?"

"*And*, she didn't know Randy a day of his life— Linda told me no one in town's ever heard of or seen her, ever."

"Well, we hardly knew him either."

"But we would give the treasure to the person it was meant for," Lily said stubbornly. "Wouldn't we?"

Jade pulled at a hangnail jutting out from her thumb. She paused for a moment and thought about Randy Banks' treasure going to someone who didn't even know him, when he had plotted a whole hunt out for someone else. "Fine."

Lily nodded proudly, already pulling open the door to Jade's room.

Margaret waved a whisk dripping with pancake batter at them as they walked past her. Her skin was blushed from the heat of the stove. "Jade, did you want another pancake?" she asked as a large glob of batter fell from the whisk onto the kitchen floor. She knelt down to wipe it off with her finger.

"I'm okay, Grandma," Jade said, grabbing a slice of bacon from the counter and ripping into it as she walked out the door. "We're going out. See you later!"

"Okay—I love you!" Margaret called out as the door slid behind them.

They walked briskly along the sidewalk. No one was awake yet except old Mrs. Girde, who was sitting on her porch, picking cat fur off of her sweater as they passed.

"I've been thinking," Lily said, moving her arms like one of the retirees on a morning walk. "The place where it all began. It has to be the graveyard, right?"

"God, I hope not," Jade said, imagining them sneaking between gravestones in the middle of the night, clad in knit black ski-masks, shovels over their shoulders.

Mrs. Girde's son walked past in a gray tracksuit, alternating between lifting two small blue weights. He breathed out in small, tight-lipped puffs, eyes fixed on the lines of the sidewalk ahead of him.

"I wonder..." Jade said after he'd passed.

"Hm?'

"It's a small town," Jade said, looking over at Lily knowingly. "If Randy Banks was seeing someone, there's no way it was just between them. And you said Linda knows things about the cousin?"

Lily paused. "You aren't suggesting we talk Linda? Not that. Please."

"She knows everything! You've said it yourself: she's the gossip hub of the whole town."

"That was supposed to be an insult," Lily said, frowning. "I have one mandatory meal with them a month. I've done my time— we can talk about this next month."

Looking at Lily, whose jaw was set out firmly, Jade decided not to push the subject any further. After all, she didn't know what it was like to have a step-parent, especially one as enthusiastic and, well, young as Linda.

Main Street was as quiet as it had been the day before. Gil was falling asleep at his counter, watching mesmerized as he slid a rag over the sud-sopped surface. Someone had gone on a flyer rampage since Jade and Lily had last visited Wide Al's; there were homemade posters proclaiming "Yard Sale!" on every lamppost. They were colored in bright crayon, like a proud five year-old was using the sale as an opportunity to share his art with the town.

As they neared Wide Al's, Jade noticed that something was reflecting the sunlight back in their direction. The glare of the reflection was so intense that they couldn't tell where it was coming from until they were mere feet away.

Jade crossed her arms as she walked towards the cherry-red car and, bending over, saw her reflection almost perfectly in the glazed paint. Inside the car, the seats were covered in cheetah-print designs. A small luau dancer stood still on the dashboard, arms frozen in the middle of her dance.

"That definitely isn't his," Lily said as they walked into Wide Al's.

Both girls froze as soon as the door swung behind them.

Eleanor Banks was leaning over the bar, her hand curled around a pen from the local dentist's office and poised over a packet of papers. Al was standing across from her, watching the pen move with apparent satisfaction.

Jade looked at Lily with wide eyes. She tried to mouth "What now?" to Lily, but Lily was hopeless at reading lips. She raised her eyebrows crookedly at Jade and moved closer to the woman, peering over her shoulder.

"Lily," Al said, flashing his eyes wide. "Give Miss Banks some space, would ya?"

Lily shuffled back, glaring at her father.

"Is this your daughter?" Ms. Banks asked, hardly looking up.

"Sure is. The older one."

Lily glared at him. She hated even the most subtle reference to her half-sister. Al didn't notice; his eyes were still fixed intently on the page. "Now, you just have to sign here, and the place is yours," he said, jutting his thick finger over a thin line printed on the bottom of the page.

Ms. Banks nodded, but her hand was frozen over the line.

"Something wrong?" Al asked. He looked as if he might reach over the counter and move the woman's hand across the page for her.

"I just wonder if I should look around first," she said, looking up at him almost pleadingly. "I know you said it's a mess right now, but I'd really rather—"

"Sure, sure, I'll give you a tour. Just sign here first," Al said. He sounded rather aggressive, and he must've realized this, because after a few seconds he emitted a nervous laugh which caught at the bottom of his throat.

Ms. Banks looked at him skeptically. She capped the pen and set it down on the paper. Al seemed to be sinking into the rotten floorboards. He started to pull at his beard anxiously.

"A quick look around," he said. "And then back to business."

Ms. Banks nodded. A great strand of hair fell out of her bun as she stood up.

"I'll start with the bathroom," she said, walking directly into the small room and shutting the door behind her.

"Start with..." Al stared blankly at the door. "How'd she even know where the bathroom was?"

"Haven't you shown her the place before?" Jade interjected.

Al's baffled expression deepened as he turned to Jade. She could understand why—she'd uttered less than ten words directly to him over the course of her friendship with Lily. She didn't like him, didn't like the devil tattoo etched into his forearm, didn't like the way he spoke to Lily.

"Of course not," Al said once he'd registered the fact that Jade had a voice.

"That doesn't make any sense," Lily said. Her tone was patronizing, and Al's face was reddening. "Why would she buy it before seeing it?"

"Because that's the only way I'd let her see it," Al said proudly. "She said she wanted a look around, and I said no one's poking around my bar so long as it's mine, and she said 'how much?'"

Before Lily could respond, Ms. Banks emerged from the bathroom. Only a few strands of hair remained tied back, and her face was flushed. She closed the door behind her quickly.

"I'll look at the backroom next," she said firmly.

"There's no backroom," Al said, eyes narrowing. "Where'd you hear there's a backroom?"

"Do you want me to buy your bar," Ms. Banks said, tugging the hair tie out of her hair once and for all. "Or not?"

"There's no back room," Lily repeated. "Really."

Al looked at Lily in surprise. Ms. Banks narrowed her eyes and crossed her arms, planting her feet farther apart.

"I'm not buying until I've seen the whole place," she said.

Al was clearly swallowing a robust series of curses. He gulped, massaged his thick red throat slowly, and nodded in defeat. "It's over there," he said, gesturing to the other doorway.

Ms. Banks pulled her thin gray cardigan closer around her and went through the second doorway, shutting the door behind her once again.

"Why's she keep shutting the door?" Al asked suspiciously. He turned to Lily. "Thanks for trying, Lil-bug."

Lily flinched at his chosen nickname but nodded. She watched the door anxiously. Meanwhile, Jade opened the bathroom door and peered inside.

"Lily," Jade said as the hinges swung with a long creak. "You should see this."

The vent cover was unscrewed, the toilet tank's cover placed on the floor, the cabinet over the sink emptied into the basin. Lily only gave the bathroom a quick glance before stomping over to the backroom door and pulling it open. Ms. Banks was standing there, hand outstretched to turn the doorknob herself.

"What did you do to our bathroom?" Lily asked.

"Lily," Al said in a half whisper. "Don't be rude. Everyone does it."

Lily swung around and gave her father an exasperated

look.

"She didn't *use* the bathroom, Dad. She searched it."

"Searched…" Al walked over to the bathroom. "What's this?"

"I was inspecting," Ms. Banks said shamelessly. "Something I clearly should have done *before* I offered to buy this dump."

"Inspecting?" Al's throat was becoming unclogged, and all of the insults he'd been saving up were on the verge of tumbling out. "*Inspecting*? This is property damage, is what this is."

"You'll find nothing broken," Ms. Banks insisted. "And, frankly, I'm the one who should be upset. This place is disgusting. There's mold between some of the boards, the backroom will take months to empty and clean, and the piping clearly hasn't been checked up on in years."

"All things that you'll take care of," Al said, marching towards the bar and grabbing the paperwork. He thrust it in her face. "Do you want it, or not?"

"Definitely not," Ms. Banks said, stepping back to avoid the paperwork. She walked directly towards the door. As Ms. Banks passed her, Jade noticed that the purse on her shoulder seemed to have grown. She leaned over a bit and saw a stack of papers. No, not papers—maps. Randy Banks' maps. The door made a loud, definitive sound as it shut behind Ms. Banks.

Chapter Eight: The Stepmother

"Of course she took them," Lily said bitterly. "Of course she didn't want to buy it. How stupid could he be?"

Lily and Jade were walking home from the bar. As soon as Ms. Banks had left, Al had walked into the backroom, slamming the door behind him. There was the sound of a collision, reminiscent of a hand punching through drywall, followed by a series of curses. Lily went into the bathroom and cleaned up what she could. Then she started toward the door.

"Shouldn't we…" Jade nodded towards the backroom.

"No," Lily said. "Let's just go."

Ms. Banks' car was already rolling down the other end of Main Street as they walked out of Wide Al's. Lily watched it go with a look of utter disgust.

"I don't think he was being stupid," Jade said softly. "She tricked him."

"He shouldn't've fallen for it," Lily said, kicking a clump of grass that was valiantly attempting to grow between two slabs of sidewalk. "He shouldn't have gotten my hopes up like that."

Jade nodded. She didn't quite know what to say. She wondered what she would do if her father owned a bar and had two arms filled with tattoos and made dumb mistakes.

Margaret had dropped a few spare details about her father in the past. When Jade had first asked, Margaret said he was a professor. A few years later, Jade asked again, but this time Margaret said she wasn't sure he was alive. One day, she brought home a research paper from school about an astronaut, and Margaret said Jade's father worked for NASA, too.

"You're not making any sense, Grandma," Jade had said, dropping the paper on the floor. "Is he a teacher or is he dead or is he on the moon?"

"Could be any of those things, really," Margaret had said forlornly. "I didn't know much about him, if I'm being honest. I don't think Caroline knew him so well either. Probably no better than your new friend's dad. What's her name again? Lauren?"

Lily hummed along to songs from the new TLC album as they walked, passing the newly awoken citizens of Paradise. The average townsperson woke up at nine o'clock, listened to the waves crash and a few spare cars roll by for the next hour, and finally left the house at noon in search of groceries or gossip. Groceries were available in only one place, a small shop on Main Street. Gossip could be found just about everywhere, but the majority of it stemmed from the woman who just happened to be walking towards them at that moment.

Linda swiftly turned the corner onto Main Street, and now she was walking at full force, white sneakers pounding against the pavement. Lily's half-sister was pulling at her mother's bright auburn hair and wailing, her chubby legs pummeling Linda in the gut. She didn't so much as flinch.

"Lily, baby!" she exclaimed as she drew closer. Lily's eyes flashed in all directions, but it was too late to find an escape. Jade wondered whether Linda had been standing at that corner all day, waiting to run into them.

"Hi, Linda," Lily said drily. She looked at the baby in her arms. "Trina."

"Silly Lil!" Linda said, beaming. "Trina can't *hear* you. She's a baby."

Lily opened her mouth to argue, but Jade knew to cut

her off. "How've you been, Linda," Jade asked, curling her cheeks up into a constipated smile.

"Oh, I have been just wonderful!" Linda said eagerly. "Little Trina baby took her first steps yesterday, and, well, I'm sure you've heard Al's—" She stopped and looked at Lily apologetically. "Your *father*'s big news."

"I know what his name is," Lily said exasperatedly, but Jade interjected again.

"We were just with him."

Linda's smile expanded. "Was Miss Banks there? I was just about to pop in and see if the deal was done."

"It isn't," Lily said bluntly.

"Well, I'm sure she'll come soon," Linda said, still smiling. "I was gonna make something nice tonight, to celebrate, if you want to come." She looked at Jade. "You too, honey."

There was something disturbing about being called "honey" by someone only fifteen years older than you. Lily was constantly making fun of Linda for it.

"She's not a waitress in a side-of-the-road diner," Lily would say. "Honey, honey, honey! Oh, it drives me crazy."

"Well," Linda asked as the silence expanded. "Will you come?"

"Ms. Banks didn't buy it, Linda," Lily said. She said it slowly, as if she were speaking to baby Trina. In fact, Linda was making the same face as Trina: wide-eyed, wide-lipped, quizzical and naïve.

"What do you mean? Al said it was all set. Just a signature to go and it was done."

"Well, she didn't buy it," Lily said. "We left just after she did."

Linda moved Trina onto her other hip. The baby leaned back precariously, but her mother pulled her closer with a carefully manicured hand.

"I'll bet she was looking for old Randy's things," she

said, narrowing her eyes suspiciously. "As soon as Al told me, I said, 'Al, don't you think there's something fishy about all this, the way old Randy dies and then she comes out of nowhere and wants to see the place where all his things were stored.' It's got to be about that gold everyone talks about, I said. It's got to be."

Lily's mouth was hanging open a bit now, too. "You really said that?" she asked skeptically.

"Sure did," Linda said sadly. "But he said it didn't matter what she wanted, so long as she paid him, and I couldn't argue with that. I told him not to let her into the backroom, though."

"You did?"

"Yes, I did. He let her in, didn't he?"

"He did," Jade said. She was just as astonished as Lily seemed to be. Linda had put together the treasure hunt without any of the clues.

"Hmph," Linda said. "He doesn't think sometimes, does he?"

"No," Lily said. "I don't think he ever does."

Linda smiled and held baby Trina closer. "I'll see you later, then, honey," she said, stepping around them and pounded her way onwards, likely to smack her husband upside the head.

Lily turned to Jade as soon as she'd walked away, seemingly impressed. "I can safely say," she said. "I did not see that coming."

Jade snorted.

"I mean, she might actually have a brain," Lily continued. "She might actually be a real, functioning human being."

"So you think we should talk to her?"

Lily looked at the sidewalk nervously. "You can't tell my mom. She hates Linda twice as much as I ever have."

"I know. We can go see her tonight."

Chapter Nine: Birthday Cake

"You're going to Al's?" Margaret yelled skeptically from the kitchen. "Al with the tattoos?"

Jade walked into the kitchen and sat on one of the barstools. On the other side of the island, Margaret was bent over a precariously stacked two-tier cake, sliding chocolate butter cream over the burnt surface.

"Yeah," Jade said, frowning. "What's this for again?"

"Caroline's birthday," Margaret said, with no further explanation.

"What?"

Margaret looked up at Jade as if she weren't understanding something very simple. "Your *mother*, Caroline. It's her birthday today."

"Wh— okay. Why are we celebrating it?"

"Because," Margaret said as she sifted a handful of sprinkles onto the uneven frosting. "I think it's time we started talking more about Caroline."

"We talk about her," Jade said, reaching over and swiping her finger against the cake, licking the icing off casually.

Margaret reached to bat her hand away without looking. Her eyes were trained on the cake, her mouth puckered close.

"Grandma, you're being weird," Jade said. "I don't want to talk about her any more than we do."

Margaret nodded hesitantly. "Take the cake with you, then," she said, procuring a large plastic platter. "For Al and Linda."

"Okay. If you don't want it."

"I hate chocolate," Margaret said sadly. She wiped her hands on her jeans, likely thinking that there was an apron hanging on top of them. There wasn't; the chocolate smeared, catching in the stiff blue rivets. "So, why are you going there?"

"Al's sad."

"Al's always sad. I thought Lily hated him. And that girlfriend of his. What's her name again?"

"Linda, and she's his wife now," Jade said. "They got married right before they had Trina."

"Trina? Lily has a sister?"

"Grandma, you've *met* her."

"Right, right, I'm sorry. Why's Al sad?"

"Randy Banks' cousin was planning on buying the bar from him, but she backed out today. Totally trashed the place looking through Randy's things," Jade said offhandedly, picking a fallen sprinkle off of the countertop and dropping it on her tongue.

"Randy's things were at the bar?" Margaret looked up from the cake.

"Yeah, I guess he didn't have enough space at home."

Margaret slanted the cake plate until the dessert flipped over onto the platter.

"Why was the cousin going through his things?"

"You won't get mad at me if I tell you, right?"

Margaret frowned.

"It's not like we're digging up flowers or anything. I'm old enough to know this is real."

"What's real?"

"Remember all the rumors about Banks? How he had gold hidden away somewhere?"

"Vulgar rumors," Margaret said. "Couldn't they let the man rest in peace?"

"Lily and I think they're true."

Margaret's forehead collapsed in on itself. "Jade, I really don't think—"

"There are real clues this time."

Margaret shook her head.

"Remember at the funeral? How he left that poem?"

"Emily Dickinson," Margaret remembered softly. "A nice touch."

"It was a *clue*."

"It was a poem, Jade." Margaret kneaded her temples with her knuckles. "You're giving me a headache." She paused. "Is this what you were using the metal detector for?"

"There was a clue in Randy's things. There were all these maps, and the only constant was the pier."

"Have you been sleeping enough?"

"What? Grandma, I'm serious. I was with Lily, she can tell you."

"She always goes along with your theories."

"It's not a theory!"

Margaret nodded, unconvinced. She folded tinfoil around the cake. Frosting shot out of the cracks in the folds.

"I'll show you," Jade said.

"Maybe later. When my head feels better."

"There was a note, from Randy. In a bottle," Jade paused, smiling. "Well, a soda can."

Margaret turned back to her. "What did it say?"

"We think Randy had a *girlfriend*," Jade said.

Margaret rolled her eyes, compressing the cracks in the tinfoil.

"We're going to ask Linda about it tonight."

"Linda? What would Linda know?"

"A lot, actually. She knows everything that happens in Paradise. She'll want to find the gold, too."

"That doesn't seem right. Shouldn't it go to family?"

"Well, that's what Lily and I were thinking. Randy made it clear in the note that he wanted his girlfriend to find it. So we're finding it to give to her."

"Show me this note, then," Margaret said. She caught herself, adding: "If there is one."

"Of course there is. I'll show you right now."

Margaret crossed her legs and waited.

"Well, it's not here," Jade said. "We put it back where we found it."

Margaret sighed. She went to the cupboard, swallowed two slick red pills for her headache, and slipped on a pair of sandals. She grabbed the first thing available on the coat rack: a bright green raincoat, for a drizzling spring afternoon. Jade smiled as the green hood went up and her grandmother opened the door. Finally, she had proof. It was not all made up in her head, and there would be no neighbor to apologize to. She took the shovel from where it was lying, packed with now-dry sand on the back porch, and swung it back over her shoulder.

Margaret walked more quickly than usual across the beach. The waves were suddenly calm. Jade wondered what was happening beneath the surface. She imagined small crabs scuttling over pebbles, minnows slipping through the current, a whale shark bobbing along in the depths. She was thinking about whale sharks when they reached the pier.

"Well?" Margaret said rather abrasively. "Where is it?"

Jade went to the post where they'd found and left the can and started to dig. Time passed, the flat heat of the sun beating against the pier's boards, and the shovel hit nothing.

"It's okay, Jade," Margaret said. "Let's just let the whole thing go, okay?"

"The cousin took it," Jade said. "She figured it out already."

"I really don't think Randy Banks' cousin is going on

treasure hunts, Jade." Margaret tied the raincoat around her waist, fanning her face limply with one hand.

"I know she is," Jade said, packing the sand back into place.

Margaret walked towards her and took her by both hands. "This is why I wanted to talk about Caroline," she said, massaging Jade's palms soothingly.

"Caroline? What does she have to do with anything?"

"I think," Margaret said slowly. "This is your way of connecting with her." She paused, leaned in to search Jade's gaze. "Am I right?"

"No," Jade said. "I don't want to connect with her any more than she does with me."

Margaret nodded, with more sympathy than agreement. "I understand," she said in an irritatingly calm voice. "I know it's odd, never seeing her."

Jade pulled her hands away. "I'm fine, Grandma. This isn't anything deep. It's just a treasure hunt."

"We've been through this enough times for me to know it's not just that."

Margaret reached out to stroke Jade's hair. Jade dodged it. She felt bad for a second, as she watched Margaret's face soften. But there was a knot in her throat, and it was expanding.

"I need to get to Al's."

"It's barely four," Margaret said, extending her arms again. "Let's walk home and talk."

"I'd rather not," Jade said. She propped the shovel back against her shoulder and started to walk.

Margaret's breathing intensified as she tried to keep up with her. "Jade, would you slow down a bit? I'm too old for these tantrums," she said, laughing lightly at herself.

Jade was not in the mood to laugh. "I'll meet you at the house," she said.

"But we're walking in the same—"

"I need space," Jade said firmly. She sped up even more. As her legs swung ahead of one another, she realized how ridiculous and petty she must seem to any onlooker: a teenage girl stomping away, in the same direction as her grandmother. But this thought only made her move faster. It was too late to turn back and apologize, and even if she did, Margaret would see this as a sign that she wanted to talk.

Jade wasn't entirely sure when it happened, but at some point her fast-walking turned into a jog, and then a sprint, and then she was pounding her thin sandal-clad feet against the sand, veering towards the right, where the dark sand clapped under her steps and the waves reached out to lick her toes. Her heart was racing, her breath coursing through her unevenly, and she was painfully aware of how long it had been since she'd really exercised.

After a couple of minutes, she stopped, bent over for a moment, felt the blood rush up to her cheeks. She looked ahead at the stretch of beach and wanted desperately to run more, but then she made the mistake of looking back. Far off, a green speck not unlike a clump of sea grass. Jade turned around and walked towards her grandmother. Neither spoke until they had reached the house.

Chapter Ten: Tattoos and Brisket

Al's home was built on stilts so thin they looked like toothpicks. Jade had little doubt that a properly motivated wave could buckle the stilts over with a single push and pull, sweeping the yellow shingles and vinyl roof into the water. She clutched the banner as they climbed the flight of stairs to the front door. Al answered the door and stared at them, dumbfounded.

"Is that Lily and Jade?" Linda called. "Let them in!"

There was a porcelain gnome at the front door, with a knobby nose and two blushed cheeks. The living room was all lace and doilies. A stitched embroidery of a bouquet of violets was hung above a fake fireplace, which had been clumsily installed and was visibly crooked compared to the floor boards; unless, of course, the floor was crooked, and the fireplace was the only thing right-side-up in the entire house.

The door to Linda and Al's bedroom was open. There were stitched pillows on a quilted bedspread, roofed with a home-made canopy: another quilt, draped over the bedposts haphazardly.

Linda was sitting at a bright white table, which was so large and bulky that it stretched across the dining room and into part of the living room. She stood up and walked to meet them, pecking Al on the cheek as if he hadn't already been there and then giving Lily an awkward side-hug. Lily didn't seem to have the energy to resist.

"Twice in one day!" Linda exclaimed. "What a treat."

"The place looks great," Jade said quietly. She couldn't even convince herself that she was telling the truth, but Linda beamed.

"It's been a lot of work, I'll tell you that," she said jovially. "When I moved in here, well, Ally hardly even washed his sheets!"

"Ally?" Lily asked. Jade could feel her friend regretting the decision to come.

"I brought cake!" Jade said a bit too enthusiastically. She thrust the platter into Linda's hands.

Linda eyed the mass of tin foil and frosting uneasily. "That's so kind of you," she said as she brought it to the kitchen.

"It's chocolate. My grandma made it," Jade flinched as she felt her voice drop into a nervous mutter.

"We didn't know you were coming," Al said, still staring blankly at Lily.

"Glad to see you, too," Lily gave him a pointed look. "I can leave if you want."

"That's not what I—"

"Don't be silly!" Linda exclaimed, beckoning them into the kitchen. "Al, I saw them earlier on my walk with Trina and invited them."

Al nodded, his eyes fixed on Lily as if she were an apparition. Jade felt a pang of sympathy for him; he seemed genuinely speechless at the thought that his daughter would willingly visit him.

"Why don't you sit down," Linda offered, pulling out a chair for Lily. "Your sister just fell asleep. Took forever to get her down."

Lily flinched at the word "sister." Jade had never heard her refer to Trina as anything other than "Trina" or "devil in a diaper."

"Do we have enough food?" Al asked, still staring at Lily.

"I made extra, just in case," Linda said.

"Thank you," Jade said, curling her cheeks back into a smile as she sat down next to Lily at the table. The longer she forced a smile, the more her cheeks shook with the effort.

"It's no problem at all," Linda said as she placed a steaming brisket in the middle of the table. She plopped a dollop of mashed potatoes, full of shredded skin and chunks of salt, on each of their plates.

"How's school?" Al asked Lily as he shoved a forkful of mashed potatoes in his mouth.

"It's summer vacation," Lily said.

Al threw his hands up mockingly. "Who's to know when these breaks are anyways?" he asked, turning to Linda for support.

Linda turned away from him and toward Lily. "What're your plans for this summer? Any fun parties coming up?"

"Not really," Lily said. "Probably just go swimming, go to the movies. That kind of stuff."

"I haven't been to the movies in so long," Linda said. Jade imagined her as a spider, clutching on to each translucent thread she could find and scuttling up it. "What's out lately?"

"Have you seen *Clueless*? We saw it last week."

They had actually seen *Clueless* twice last week, the second time dressed up in their most Cher-like outfits: plaid on plaid on chunky heels that Lily found in her mother's closet. Both girls loved to watch such a perfect-seeming girl mess up over and over again. Sure, she had the closet of their dreams, but boy was her taste in men off.

"It humanizes her," Lily had explained as they sat in the back of the theater, biting down on mouthfuls of popcorn and fishing the kernels out of their back teeth.

Al grunted as he served himself a plateful of brisket.

"We see movies plenty," he said, cutting out a mouthful and wiping a smear of mashed potatoes on top of it.

"I love Indiana Jones," Linda continued. "Harrison Ford is—"

Linda gave Lily and Jade what appeared to be intended as a knowing look. Al looked up from his brisket in disapproval, hesitated, and then looked back down.

"You know," Linda said. "Your dad got a new tattoo."

"That's cool."

"You think so?" Al said, looking up.

"Yeah, I'm sure it's great," Lily said. She was only half paying attention, eyes fixed on her plate.

"Do you wanna see it?"

"Sure."

Without warning, Al reached down and pulled up his shirt, so that it balled up under his neck. He strained to look down at his chest. Lily looked up, still disinterested. Her eyes widened.

Seared across Al's chest were three faces. Linda's face was planted in the middle. The tattoo artist must have gotten tired halfway through, because the right side of her face wavered, and her nose bulged out unnaturally. Jade could see from Linda's face that she was not a fan of this depiction of her. On tattoo-Linda's left side, baby Trina was immortalized mid-giggle. On her right, distinguishable through the white-blonde hair, green eyes, and sharp chin, tattoo-Lily smiled across the table at real Lily. A tuft of chest hair grew just next to her face.

Jade watched Lily's facial expressions intently; as did Al. He kept the shirt tucked under his chin, looking down at the tattoo, up at Lily, and then back down again. When she didn't respond for a while, Linda cut in.

"What do you think? We got it last weekend."

Jade could see her friend squeezing her hands together under the table. Would she laugh, or would she yell?

Somehow, Lily kept her face immobile as she stared down the tattoo version of herself and responded. "That's nice of you, Dad."

Al beamed and finally lowered his shirt back over his chest. "She likes it," he said to Linda, as if she hadn't been there.

Linda smiled at Lily, who was now digging her fingernails into her palms to keep from laughing. "I'm so glad. Because we wanted you to know," Linda glanced at Al. "That you're a part of this family, and you're always welcome here."

Lily's fingernails went deeper into her palms. "Okay," she said. "Thanks."

Linda could tell she'd gone too far. She backtracked into her go-to dinner topic. "Did you hear about Molly Werner?"

"Molly? What happened to her?" Jade asked. She'd sat next to her in Biology freshman year.

"Pregnant," Linda said gleefully. "At seventeen!"

"Crazy," Lily said. She readied her knife to cut out a new piece of brisket, but there was no more food in her plate to cut. She reached to drink from her glass instead, but Linda beat her to it, spouting out her question so quickly that the words seemed to be tumbling out of her and spilling across the table.

"Do you know her?"

"Nope," Lily said, and quickly brought the glass to her lips.

The table grew silent for a few moments, save for the sounds of Al chewing. Linda cleared her throat; Al gulped down another bite. Jade thought of different ways to pose her question. When the silence had become unbearable, she gave up and put it as bluntly as she could.

"Linda," she said shyly. Linda looked up at her. "Did you know Randy Banks well?"

"I've had enough of Randy Banks and the whole Banks family for one day," Al said roughly.

Linda ignored him again. "I didn't know him personally, but Al did," she said slowly. It was clear she was trying to build the suspense. "And from what he's told me, Randy was a real character."

"How so?" Jade prompted her.

"He was a nice guy," Al interrupted.

"Nice guy, maybe. But a weird guy." Linda turned to Jade, excited. "One time, Al went in to check on him, and he was drawing on the walls!"

"The walls?"

"Sure as day! He was scribbling all sorts of nonsense."

"Like what?" Lily asked, perking up.

"Al said he wrote—"

"That's not right, Lin," Al interjected. "He was a good man, minded his own business—"

"Writing on your *walls*!" Linda said exaggeratedly, turning to Lily and Jade and laughing loudly. They laughed awkwardly in unison.

"That's crazy!" Lily said encouragingly.

Linda nodded, proud of herself. "I'll bet," she said, her voice dropping almost to a whisper, as if anyone outside of the dining room could hear them above Al's loud chewing. "He was writing out *clues*."

"Not this again," Al said.

"Well, dontcha think?" Linda insisted, turning to Lily and Jade for affirmation. They nodded. "See, they see, there's something to it!"

"There's nothing to it!" Al said, his voice rising almost to a yell. Clearly, he hadn't intended to respond so loudly, because he blushed as soon as they fell silent. The silence only lasted for a moment, however, before baby Trina's wails took over the house.

Linda put her fork and knife down and glared at Al.

"Oh, you've got to be kidding me," she exclaimed.

"I'll get her, I'll get her," Al said. He put together one last bite while Linda continued to glare at him, shoved it in his mouth, and lumbered over to their bedroom. As soon as he had shut the door behind him, Linda turned back to Lily and Jade.

"He was writing all sorts of things," she said quickly, her voice lowering even further. "Al said he saw a bunch of numbers, five circles with arrows pointing to each other. When Randy saw him, he got angrier than Al ever saw him. Called him a snoop, a deadbeat. They were friends up until then. That's why Al doesn't like to talk about—"

Al walked out of the room with Trina lying in his arms. He was humming something familiar to Jade, but she couldn't quite pinpoint what it was. Lily started to open her mouth, presumably to ask Linda what the circles said, but Linda shook her head. She turned to Al and smiled broadly.

"Look how you calm her down! Such a natural dad."

Chapter Eleven: Robin

"Five circles," Lily said as they walked back down the precarious toothpick staircase. "That means we're close."

"How's that?"

"We've gone through four clues now. The poem, the coordinates, the maps, and pier. There's got to be one more place left, and that's where the treasure is."

It was dark outside, so Linda had given them a flashlight for the walk back. They followed the circle of yellowish light two blocks down, so they could walk on the beach. A seagull glared at them in the dark, ducking away from the light.

"We're still not any closer to the fifth clue, though," Lily said sadly. "So that was not only traumatizing, but a monumental waste of time."

"I don't think so," Jade said. "It seems like your dad wants to spend time with you."

"Linda wants my dad to want to spend time with me," Lily said. "It's an important distinction."

Jade nudged her friend lightly. "I think he's trying, Lil. That's what the tattoo was for."

"No," Lily laughed. "The tattoo was to keep me from ever looking in the mirror again."

They laughed deep-belly laughs until they were both out of breath. Jade stopped suddenly. "I think we should go to Randy Banks' house."

"Why?"

"It's worth checking." Jade said. A theory was forming

in her mind like a sandcastle, wet sand clumping and smoothing into a discernible mold. "Maybe that's the place where it all began."

Neither girl was willing to venture into the swampy Banks acre in the dark, so they went their separate ways, Jade heading towards her grandmother, Lily towards her mother. As Jade approached her peach-colored home, edges fuzzy in the velvet black, she made out the outline of Margaret, standing perfectly upright on the last step of the porch.

"Grandma?" Jade's eyes narrowed to accustom to the darkness.

"Oh," Margaret said, and immediately it was as if her lungs had been strung back into place. She heaved a great sigh, her posture collapsing and face planting itself between her palms. "Oh, thank you, God."

"What's wrong?" Jade reached out to stroke her grandmother's arm. Margaret whimpered and gathered Jade into a tight hug. She smelled like baking and musky rosebud perfume. She shook there for a moment, her tears drenching Jade's shirt, and then straightened herself to look Jade in the eyes.

"Come inside," she said, nodding along with herself. "I'll make you hot chocolate."

In the kitchen, Margaret filled a pot with milk, her back turned to Jade. The oven clicked as violet flames burst out to lick the metal.

"Grandma, what's happening?" Jade said, eyes fixed on the flames. They turned orange as they reached further upwards.

Margaret turned around. She had been wearing a thick layer of mascara before she'd started crying, and now it streaked the bags under her eyes in dark clumps.

"I just got scared, honey."

"Not just tonight," Jade pushed. "You've been off for a

while now."

"I just…" Margaret turned away from Jade again as she reached for the hot chocolate mix in the top cupboard. Her fingers flailed upwards like the flames. "I can't reach. Can you get it?"

Margaret leaned against the counter as Jade reached to grab the mix. Jade could feel her grandmother watching her intensely. Margaret cleared her throat.

"I get scared of losing you," she said softly, her voice inverting on itself. "I get really scared of that sometimes."

"Losing me?" Jade set the hot chocolate powder down on the counter. "How would you lose me?"

"Just…" Margaret paused. "Growing up, and things like that. You're like…" She pointed to a painting of a young robin taking its first leap from the nest. "Well, I bought that painting because it reminded me of you. You're my little bird, but you'll be able to fly soon. And I don't know where you'll go."

"Is this about college? Lily and I have already decided we're applying to in-state only. You wouldn't believe how cheap—"

"Not just college."

"What, then?"

Margaret opened her mouth and emitted a light croaking noise, as if she were stuck on the first syllable of a word. Then she closed her lips together tightly, turned to the now boiling milk, and started to mix in the hot chocolate powder.

"It was easier when you were younger," Margaret said. "Don't you think?"

"I guess," Jade said. "But just because I can leave doesn't mean I will. I'll still be around, Grandma. I won't be like Mom, if that's what you're scared of."

Margaret nodded and squeezed her eyes shut, as if she were looking at something outside of the kitchen, outside of

Paradise. Jade was used to this feeling, of not seeing what her grandmother did.

"Thank you," Margaret said. "For saying that."

Jade gave her grandmother a hug and poured them two cups of hot chocolate. They sat down on the slouching couch, balancing their mugs on their knees. The television turned on in rays of green and blue and purple and red. There was a moment of static, snow piling onto the screen, and then the movie *Freaky Friday* started to play.

Jade looked over at her grandmother at different points in the movie. She never smiled or laughed at the scenarios. At the end, though, she was smiling. Jade watched her, wondered what it would be like if they traded places for a day.

"You don't have to be my mom," Jade said as the credits started to roll. She looked at the painting of the baby robin. "It's not your fault she… flew off." Jade smiled, hoping to sugarcoat the bitterness that had crept into her voice.

Margaret nodded and tucked Jade's hair behind her ears. "I could've been better with her," she said.

This was the first time Jade heard her grandmother speak of fault in her relationship with Caroline. She opened her mouth to ask what she meant, but Margaret was already kissing her on the cheek, leaving another crimson imprint, and drifting up the stairs.

Jade fell asleep on the couch that night, with the TV still glowing in front of her. She dreamt of falling out of a nest, hitting the ground, eggs cracked all around her, and then her grandmother swooped in, carried her back into the twisted bowl of twigs and leaves and tucked her to bed.

Chapter Twelve: Dead Man's Mail

"She said you were a bird?" Lily asked skeptically the next day at noon, as she and Jade started towards Randy Bank's house.

"Yeah," Jade said. She turned and saw Lily's cheeks puffed out with a withheld laugh. "Oh, come on."

"I don't get her," Lily said. "You know I love Marge, but honest to God I don't get half of what she says."

"It makes sense to me. She's just really honest, and sometimes it comes out weird, you know?"

"Sure," Lily said as she came to a stop. "It's here, Jade."

In the distance, Jade could see the clay and stucco house towering between the swamp trees. In front of her, the Banks mailbox poked jauntily out of the underbrush, marking the beginning of the winding gravel drive. It was corroded to the point of disrepair, with gaping, rust-ringed holes dotting its exterior. The side of the mailbox once said "Banks," but now it looked more like "B nl s." It was unhinged, smiling at Jade with a mouth full of magazines.

The mailbox couldn't have been as old as Thomas Banks, but Jade still imagined that it was he who had installed it, pounding it into the ground and looking around him to see no one else for miles. She often fantasized about an empty Paradise. It was already empty in a way, filled with people who seemed to be there only in passing and beach houses that were constantly being sold to pay for inlanders' divorces. But a really empty town— no houses, no pier, no people— just the seagulls and the ocean, and maybe Lily and Margaret when Jade was feeling up to social interaction. That was Jade's dream.

"Look at this," Lily said, bringing Jade out of her historical fantasy. She grabbed a stack of magazines from the mailbox and started to thumb through the glossy pages.

"Lily!" Jade exclaimed. "Put those down."

Jade looked around the neighborhood. The only person she could see was an old man sitting at his porch, arms crossed firmly like a sheriff's in a wild west movie. The effect was dampened by his open, drooling mouth.

"Look, the Washington zoo got a baby panda," Lily said, holding a copy of National Geographic up to Jade's nose. A worm-like animal with puffed pink eyes was plastered across the cover. "Isn't he cute?"

"Put them away and let's hurry," Jade said. She was beginning to feel annoyed with Lily.

"Fine, fine."

As Lily reached to stuff the magazines back into the mailbox, an envelope slid out from between them. Jade bent to pick it up. RETURN TO SENDER, the top of it yelled through a bold red stamp. Jade read the rest of the envelope despite herself. Her eyes flickered to the middle of the rectangle. Smack dab in the middle, in scrawling cursive but still as clear as could be: *Caroline Adelson*.

"What the—" Jade's whisper trailed off.

Lily leaned over to see. Her eyebrows rose sharply. "What was Randy doing, writing to your mom?"

"This doesn't make sense," Jade said to herself.

She rubbed the address on the envelope, as if to check that it was real. The dark blue ink didn't budge. 23 Old Bay Court, Willow Bend, North Carolina. Willow Bend, North Carolina. A fishing town twenty minutes from Paradise. Jade went there once on a school field trip. She smelled like fish guts when she came back, and Margaret made her shower three times to get rid of the smell.

"It says return to sender," Lily suggested limply. "Maybe she used to stay there, a long time ago, and Randy got that address for some reason?" She searched Jade's face. "Or maybe she has a PO box in Willow Bend."

"Who has a PO box in Willow Bend?" Jade asked.

It was as if her heart had slipped through her chest and landed in the pit of her stomach, where it was now being jostled around between her organs. She wanted to rip the letter open, but somehow it seemed wrong to open it in front of Lily. She wished she could teleport to her room, crawl under her bed, and slowly undo the seal.

"We need to go there," Jade said, stuffing the letter into her pocket. "To Willow Bend."

"I don't think that's a good idea," Lily said, reaching towards Jade's pocket. "Come on, let's put the letter back, and we'll go talk to Margaret."

"I don't," Jade wished her heart would go back in its place. " I don't think I trust her right now."

Lily opened her mouth to argue, and then thought better of it. "Okay," she said. "We'll go tomorrow morning, once you've had some time to calm down."

"No," Jade said. Her heart was clawing at her insides. "We have to go today. I need to know what's happening."

"Let's put the letter back at least," Lily said, lowering her voice. "It's not like we can open it."

"Hey, there!" The retiree was summoned back to waking reality. He stood up slowly and squinted at them from across the street. "What are you girls doing? Don't touch a dead man's mail!"

"Let's go," Lily said. "Before he calls the police or something."

Now it was Jade who walked ahead. She tried to focus on the beating of her sneakers against the concrete, to match her heartbeat with it, but that didn't work.

Everything around her was blurry and wrong.

Her mother was in Willow Bend, or at least she had some connection to it. What did this mean? That she was not in Costa Rica, hunting for a lost kingdom, or in England, bartering for a crown jewel? That she was actually here, in North Carolina, just next to her daughter and mother? Why would Randy Banks know that? What connection could he have to Jade's mother? Caroline had never lived in Paradise. She had never visited, never called, never so much as written a letter. And Margaret. Did she know about this mysterious address in Willow Bend? Jade's mind was cluttered and pulsing. She walked faster.

Chapter Thirteen: The Boy on the Bicycle

Lily pushed hard on the car key as she twisted it into the ignition. She squinted at the rearview mirror and stomped down on the gas, sending the muddy red pickup truck down the driveway and onto the main road. Lily's mother watched from the front door, close to tears with anxiety.

"How'd you convince her?" Jade asked, reaching to hold onto the door handle.

"I told her I had my license, and if she didn't let me drive, I'd walk."

"To Willow Bend?"

"Yeah. Glad she didn't call my bluff?"

"She would've if she knew how many tries it took you to get that license."

Lily had spent all spring practicing for her driver's test. After school, every day for a month, she and Jade would go out to their high school's parking lot, plant orange cones around parking spots, and practice. Once, Lily hit, or, as she put it, "nudged" their American History teacher. He was good natured about it, especially considering how he had spilled his coffee all over his shirt. By some miracle, Lily passed on her third try. She said the examiner was too hungover to care that she blew through a stop sign.

"I'm really not so bad," Lily said, swinging a hard left. The car next to them slammed down on their horn as she cut into their lane. The truck's balance shifted alarmingly. "Do you know where we're going?"

Jade unfolded the map from Lily's house, the same map they'd used to find the clue that led them to Wide Al's. She traced her finger along the route and dictated as they went. Soon, they had left Paradise, and then they were gliding along the backroads, fringed with sweet gums and hickories. Lily popped in a cassette — Madonna— and started to sing along. The car moved jerkily, swinging in and out of the lane as she swung with the music. Jade thought for a moment of what it would be like to die in a car accident with Madonna singing "Like a virgin." How ironic.

They drove through Willow Bend's Main Street, which managed somehow to be even more depressing than the one in Paradise. A man with a fish stand— salmon laid out on ice chips— glared at them as they passed, as if they were after his produce.

They reached 23 Old Bay Court much sooner than Jade had anticipated. Lily parked the car. It bounced for a moment, and Madonna's voice fizzled out.

"How are you feeling?" Lily asked.

Jade stared at the house blankly. It was a "square" person's house, as Margaret would say. The panels were glossy plastic, the lawn perfectly cropped. There was a wind chime by the front door; it glinted in the sunlight. Jade inhaled sharply when she saw it. *It's just a wind chime,* she chided herself. *Stop jumping to conclusions*.

A pack of elementary school-aged kids rode by on their bicycles. Jade made eye contact with one of them, a scrawny red-haired boy with cupped pads on his knees and elbows. He smiled at her, riding past the window before she could smile back. Jade wished she could be invisible. That she could walk through walls, walk into this perfectly manicured house and find out what was happening inside without having to talk to anyone.

"Take your time," Lily said. "But we're starting to look a little like stalkers."

Jade nodded and reached for the car door handle. She paused. "What do I do if she's in there?"

"I don't know," Lily said bluntly. "But I'll be there with you."

The boys on bicycles circled through the court, cutting past Jade and Lily as they walked across the pavement and up the walkway. The boy with red hair broke from the group as he saw them move towards the door. "Hey! No one's home right now," he said. "They're both at work."

"Thanks," Lily said. She turned to Jade. "They? I guess it's not her then."

"Who's they?" Jade asked the boy. "Is this your house?"

"I'm not supposed to talk to strangers," the boy said matter-of-factly.

"Well, you already are," Lily pointed out.

"Be diplomatic," Jade whispered, elbowing her friend gently. She turned back to the boy. "I'm looking for someone."

"Mysterious," the boy said sarcastically.

"Caroline Adelson," Jade continued. "Does she live around here?"

"Nope," the boy said nonchalantly, leaning onto the bike's handlebars.

One of his friends broke from the pack. "Elliot, hurry up," the boy said as he rode towards them. "We're gonna go to the park. Sam says the ice cream truck's parked there."

"Aw, sweet," Elliot beamed. "Hey, do you know a Caroline Adelson?"

"No," the boy said. He thought for a moment. "Isn't your mom's name Caroline?"

"*Step-mom*," Elliot said adamantly. "And her last name's Gordon, idiot."

"People's last names *change*, fart-wad," the boy said.

"C'mon, we're going."

Elliot turned back to Jade and Lily and shrugged. "Hope you find her," he said. Then he spun the bike around, started pumping his legs, and sped out of the court.

Lily turned to Jade cautiously. "Do you think it's her?"

"Who?" Jade said numbly, even though she knew exactly what Lily was saying.

"That boy's step-mom. Do you think it's your Caroline?"

"She isn't my anything," Jade said suddenly. "Let's go back."

"What?"

"Let's go back. This was stupid."

They walked back to the car in silence and rode through Main Street, past the fish and the stink and the lonely buildings, in silence. Jade watched outside despite herself, squinting to make out the faces of the women they passed. *Stupid*, she thought to herself. *Stupid, stupid, stupid.* When she closed her eyes and leaned against the window, she saw Caroline in her pink taffeta prom dress, clapping and smiling while Elliot biked in circles around her.

Chapter Fourteen: Fallen Spaghetti

When Jade got home, the daylight was already dimming. She could hear slow jazz sounding from inside the house before she'd even opened the door. Margaret was in the kitchen, chopping onions. She was turned away from the cutting board, but her eyes were still beginning to well.

"How was your day?" she asked, fanning her eyes, as Jade walked in. "Did you go swimming?"

Jade looked down at her dry outfit and dry hair. "Sure," she said. "We went swimming."

"I'm making spaghetti Bolognese," Margaret said proudly. "Your favorite."

Jade ran up the stairs two steps at a time. She lay down on her bed like a starfish, arms and legs hanging limply over the edges. There was a crack on her ceiling. As a young child, she had often worried that it would blossom until it consumed her entire room, and then everything came crashing down. This was what she felt like, lying on her bed at that moment. Like she was lying in the dark, helpless as she watched a crack slither its way across the plaster, heaving out the guts of the house.

Nina Simone's voice trembled as she hit the final note of her song. Jade sat up and took off her jacket. Margaret was dicing tomatoes; there was a dull thud each time the knife hit the cutting board. Jade reached her hand into her jacket and pulled out the envelope. Her hands felt weak, as if the envelope were filled with lead. But it wasn't. It was just a slip of paper, with another slip of paper inside. Jade reminded herself of this as she sliced open the lip with her thumbnail. Downstairs, Margaret hummed along with the music.

Dear Caroline,

My name is Randy Banks. I live in Paradise, North Carolina, not so far from you. It's funny—I've been searching for you for sixteen months now, but I never thought you would be in my own backyard.

You're probably wondering why I'm contacting you. The fact is that I love your mother and daughter very much. And, like you, I've been estranged from both of them for a while now.

When I learned the truth about you, I was living with them. Jade was four. She called me Grandpa Randy back then. I loved her, and love her very much, as I'm sure you do too. But when I learned that you weren't really a treasure hunter, I felt like a fool. A grown man, living a child's fantasy. I couldn't understand why Margaret wouldn't give you another chance. We had a falling out, and I haven't been a part of either of their lives since then.

One month ago, I learned that I am going to die. I have some time, but not nearly as much as I'd like. I don't think it's fair to ask Margaret to let me back into her life just before I go. So instead, I'm leaving her with two parting gifts. One of them is this letter. I am begging you to come to Paradise and speak to your mother. I know that she is ready to let you back in, even if she's too scared to admit it. And I know that this is what's right for Jade, who I still love like family.

With all my best wishes,
Randy Banks

Jade's eyes flew across the lines of scrawling handwriting, each word sparking a new question. Her hands shook as she read the line "A grown man, living in a child's fantasy," over and over again.

"Jade!" Margaret called from the kitchen. "Dinner's

almost ready. Will you come set the table?"

Jade stared at the quilt on her bed. She wanted nothing more than to go into the kitchen, thrust the letter in Margaret's face, and force her to explain. But her body was rooted to the bed, her eyes to the quilt. She got up slowly, easing herself down the stairs as if she were just waking up.

Margaret was grating cheese over the pasta; it fell in delicate, translucent curls. She looked up as she pushed the block of cheese further into the metal. "What's wrong?" She looked down at the letter in Jade's hand. "What's that?"

"It's a letter," Jade said. She sat down at the table.

"Oh, that's nice," Margaret said as she picked up the bowls of pasta and walked towards Jade. "I feel like people never send letters anymore. Who's it from?"

"Randy Banks."

There was a sharp crash, merged with an almost comical plop, as the bowls of spaghetti fell out of Margaret's hands. She looked down blankly at the spilled food, the red sauce splattered up to her ankles.

"What do you mean, Randy Banks?" She said feebly, eyes still fixed on the steaming noodles.

"He was looking for Caroline," Jade continued. Margaret looked pitiful in her bright red apron, dinner ruined in front of her, but somehow this made Jade even angrier with her. "Caroline, as in my mom. As in the woman who lives in Willow Bend, twenty minutes from here?"

"Wh—"

"She's not a treasure hunter, she's not this great, adventurous person." Jade paused. She wondered how she hadn't started crying yet. "She just didn't want me."

Margaret moved towards the table with her eyes fixed in front of her. She pulled up a chair next to Jade and reached out to hold her granddaughter's hand, but Jade pulled away.

"Why would you do this?" Jade asked, as she finally began to cry. "Why would you lie?"

Margaret was silent. The only sounds in the house were of Jade's heaving breaths and the reverberations of a piano, skipping nimbly from one note to another.

Margaret's eyes welled up as she cleared her throat. "Please," she said. "Please let me explain."

"That's what I'm asking you to do!" Jade exclaimed, wiping her eyes with the palms of her hands and looking up to glare at her grandmother.

Margaret nodded quickly. She looked past Jade's shoulder while she spoke.

"You're right," she said. "Caroline isn't a treasure hunter." Margaret paused. "I'm not sure what she is now. But I promise you, I didn't know she was living in Willow Bend. I wasn't even sure if she was, well, alive."

Jade turned away from her grandmother as she listened, eyes fixed on their fallen dinner.

"When you were three months old, the court transferred custody to me," Margaret said, her voice small. "Three months after that, I moved us here."

"Why?"

"She's an addict, Jade," Margaret said.

"You're lying to me again. I saw her house. She's married and she has a perfect little house." Jade couldn't breathe, thinking about that perfect house.

"Maybe she's better now," Margaret said. "But she wasn't then. I'm telling you the truth. Back in New York, I walked in on her passed out in front of you a handful of times. You weren't eating right, you weren't even babbling. You were silent, all the time. I told her," Margaret took a deep breath. "I told her I couldn't let my granddaughter grow up like that, but she wouldn't accept treatment. And then one night it got so much worse.

She'd seen your dad out with another woman. He'd

left her before you were born, and seeing him just about broke her. It was your three-month birthday," Margaret said, tearing up. "And when I came to visit, I found you both passed out on the living room floor."

Jade's chest was expanding like a sponge, filling and filling until she felt like she might burst. "Passed out?"

"I assumed the worst," Margaret whispered. "So I called an ambulance. It turned out you hadn't eaten in over a day. She just… forgot, I guess. She wasn't cruel, Jade, and I wish I could tell you about her when she was younger. But she'd changed; she couldn't think about you as much as she had to. The court gave her probation—"

"Probation?"

"Yes. And they gave me custody of you." Margaret stopped talking.

Jade's throat was dry, but she couldn't feel the rest of her body. The record spun through its last groove and the house fell silent. There was no wind, no wind chimes to cloak the sounds of the seagulls outside.

"Did she…" Jade swallowed. "Did she try to fight it?"

Margaret nodded. "I told her I would let her see you, no matter what the court said, but she saw me as her enemy. She spiraled, kept coming to my apartment at night and threatening to burn down the building, steal you back and disappear. After a few months, I had enough. I wouldn't let her put you in danger again. I brought you here."

Jade stood up, still clutching the letter in her hand. She put it on the table in front of Margaret, who was watching her intently. Then she started towards the door.

"Where are you going?"

Jade turned back one more time. "And Randy," Jade said. "You were together? He— he lived here?"

Margaret nodded. She stood up and started towards her. Her arms were outstretched, ready to envelop Jade in a hug.

"No," Jade said, shaking her head. "Why wouldn't you just tell me? Why wouldn't you tell me *all* of this?"

"I thought it was easier," Margaret whispered.

"For you, maybe," Jade spit out, opening the back door and stepping through it. She could hardly get the words out. "Not for me."

Chapter Fifteen: Thin Mints

"Where'd she get the idea, do you think?" Lily asked that night, as she and Jade lay side by side in Lily's bed. "To say your mom was a treasure hunter?"

"Dunno," Jade said. Her face was blotchy from hours of crying into Lily's pillowcase. She'd walked straight there and spouted the truth to Lily as soon as the bedroom door had closed. Lily had listened quietly, allowing Jade to answer her own questions and affirm her own angers. Then she'd tucked Jade into bed and gotten them both hot cocoa.

"You'll sleep here tonight," she'd said as she kicked the bedroom door shut behind her, whipped cream shaking perilously atop two ceramic mugs. "And as long as you need to."

"I guess I can, well, see where she was coming from," Lily said. Jade could tell that she'd been holding this in for some time. "Not with the lying, of course, but with taking you away. It sounds like your mom—"

"Please don't," Jade said, rolling to face the wall.

"Okay," Lily said. "I'm sorry."

"I want to see her."

"Of course you do."

"Tomorrow."

"Tomorrow? Are you sure you're ready?"

"Tomorrow."

They left before breakfast, Lily glancing at the coffee machine forlornly as they walked out the door. She scribbled a note for her mom and left it on the fridge. *Gone with Jade. Back later.*

Jade had spent her night playing out the different scenarios that could be waiting for her at 23 Old Bay Court. She'd imagined her mother swinging open the door, searching Jade's face for just a moment and then shuddering as if a ghost had walked through her. She had imagined her beaming, pulling Jade into her arms, introducing her to her new father and brother. She'd imagined the door swung back in her face, her step-brother staring at her cluelessly from the window.

"She's no one," Jade imagined Caroline saying, pulling Elliot from the window. "Don't tell your father."

As Lily's car swung across the bends of the road, a new possibility popped into Jade's mind. What if Caroline from Willow Bend wasn't Jade's Caroline? What if Randy Banks had found the wrong Caroline, and the real one was still in New York City, doing all the things Margaret had described? Jade bit the inside of her cheek, where a blister had been festering ever since she'd found Randy's letter the day before.

The sun was beating down on Willow Bend on this particular day. Ice chips stacked over fish scales were melting rapidly. A group of girls in bathing suits and large t-shirts walked across the street in front of Lily's car, towels slung over their shoulders. This was the warmest day of the summer, and Jade couldn't stop shivering.

Lily parked in the same place she'd parked the day before, just across from 23 Old Bay Court. Once again, they sat in silence, eyes locked on the house. The curtains were open, but the glare of the sunlight obscured the inside of the house from view. Jade squinted, half expecting her mother to open the front door at any moment. The silence continued. Jade inhaled as deeply as she could and opened the car door. She turned back to Lily, who was unbuckling her seat belt.

"Is it okay if I go alone?"

"I'll be here," Lily said, smiling encouragingly.

Jade hesitated again when she reached the door. Her hand hung in the air, fist clenched and ready to knock. She noticed that the door had been painted recently. It was a bold red, the color of lipstick smudges, with no chipping or cracking. Jade was suddenly afraid to touch this perfect door. She started to turn around when a gust of wind blew through Old Bay Court. The wind chime next to her started to sing. Jade knocked.

Someone called out from within the house, and there was the sound of footsteps beating against a staircase, reaching the platform, walking slowly towards the door. A man with a speckled face and crop of bright white hair opened the door.

"Thanks, young lady, but I have twenty boxes of Thin Mints in my pantry," he said, before the door had stopped swinging.

Jade's jaw unlocked. What was there to say to this?

"We don't need any more," he added, and started to close the door.

"I'm not a Girl Scout," Jade started to say, but she was mumbling. The door closed. "Wait!" Jade exclaimed. She knocked on the door again, and the man opened it. His ears were tipped with red.

"I'm sorry, but we just can't take any more cookies," he continued.

"I'm not a Girl Scout."

"Oh," the man said. "I'm so sorry. There must have been a hundred Girl Scouts by here in the last two days and, well, frankly they're more aggressive than you'd think."

"It's fine," Jade said, because she didn't know what else to say.

"Who are you, then?" the man asked. The door swung open a bit more, and Jade saw that he was leaning on a cane. "One of Elliot's friends?" Without waiting for Jade to respond, he swung his head back and yelled out. "Elliot!"

"No," Jade said. "No, I'm not one of Elliot's friends. Please just listen to me."

The man frowned.

"I'm looking for Caroline," Jade continued. "Caroline Adelson. Is she here?"

"How do you know Carol?"

"I'd really like to speak with her."

"Well, I'd really like to marry Cindy Crawford, but that hasn't happened, has it? How do you know my daughter-in-law?"

Jade opened her mouth to speak when she saw two kitten heels click onto the top step of the stairs. As the heels clicked farther down, she saw a skirt, then an olive sweater, then the face of her mother, decades older and covered in blotches of foundation that smeared around the edges of her soft jawline. Even from afar, Jade could see the clumps of mascara between her eyelashes.

"Henry?" Caroline asked. "Did you tell her we don't want any more cookies?"

Jade was rooted on the doorstep. The wind revived itself for a moment, and the chime followed its tune.

"Sweetie, we just don't need—" Caroline broke off as she made eye contact with Jade.

"Alright," Henry said, leaning heavily on his cane as he turned back and forth between Caroline and Jade. "What's goin' on here?"

"Jade?" Caroline asked weakly, ignoring him.

Jade nodded. Her mother nodded in return, biting down so hard on her bottom lip that she scraped a layer of lipstick off. She didn't move.

"How did you find me?" she asked.

"Randy Banks."

"Who?" Caroline looked down at the floor, racked her brain. "It doesn't matter. Come in. Please, come in."

Chapter Sixteen: Behind the Curtain

Jade stepped into the house and Henry shut the door behind her. She wondered what Lily was thinking, watching from the car as the door opened, closed, opened, and finally let her in. What was Jade thinking? She wasn't sure of that, either. All she knew was that she wanted her mother to hug her, to say something more, but Caroline seemed paralyzed.

"Why don't we sit down," Henry suggested. "Carol, you look pale."

"I'm fine," Caroline whispered. "Henry, would you leave us?"

Henry hesitated, and Jade could tell that he wasn't used to unexplained situations.

But Caroline's face was firm. "Please," she added weakly.

"Sure, sure," he said finally , turning to climb back up the staircase.

Caroline walked into the adjoining living room slowly and sat down on a wide couch with patterns of ivy sewn across it. She watched Jade the entire time: as she walked, as she sat, as she gestured for her to come sit next to her.

"You must hate me," Caroline whispered as Jade lowered herself slowly to sit on the other end of the couch. Caroline crossed and uncrossed her hands on her lap. She twisted the gold ring on her index finger as if suddenly aware of its presence.

"No," Jade said. "I don't think so."

Caroline smiled quickly, but her eyebrows were drawn

into a tight V-shape, and she watched the carpet as if it had just given her a very difficult math problem.

Jade's eyes, meanwhile, drifted to the mantle. It was cluttered with framed pictures. One of a child, probably Elliot, face nestled against a croqueted blanket. Another of Caroline and a tall man with auburn hair and a thick beard.

"Is that your husband?" Jade asked, hungry for Caroline's voice.

"Yes, that's Fred," Caroline said detachedly. "We got married last summer."

"What's he do?"

"He's the mayor of Willow Bend."

"That's nice," Jade said. All her life, she had felt an emptiness that she thought this moment would fill. But with every passing second, she wondered if emptiness was something permanent. She remembered the stash of letters in her bedroom and felt a flash of anger. "Who was my father?"

Caroline flinched. "He's a lawyer in New York. Quite successful now, I hear." Her eyes remained fixed on the carpet, flitting from one side of the room to the other.

"Mom," Jade pressed. "Look at me."

Caroline shook her head slightly. She tilted her head towards Jade slightly.

"Why won't you?" Jade asked.

"I'm just… so sorry, Jade. I'm so, so sorry."

"You should have tried harder," Jade said. "You shouldn't have let me believe you didn't want me."

"You're right."

"Did you?" Jade pressed. "Want me?"

Finally, Caroline's eyes met Jade's. She reached her hand up to cup Jade's cheek, and finally Jade felt connected to her. Then a car door slammed from outside the house. Caroline started. She rushed to the window, then turned back to Jade. She opened her mouth to say something, but before she could, the front door opened. The man from the pictures on the mantle walked into the hallway.

"Fred!" Caroline exclaimed, walking up to him. "How was your day?"

"Tiring," Fred said, shrugging off his coat and flinging it over the bannister. He made it halfway up the stairs before he noticed Jade sitting on the living room couch. "Who's this?"

Jade looked at Caroline, who stared blankly at Fred.

"This is Jade," she started, her lower lip trembling. "She's—she's a Girl Scout."

"You told her we didn't want any more cookies?"

"Y—" Caroline hesitated, glanced at Jade pleadingly.

"Good," Fred said. He turned back to the staircase and walked up.

Jade stood up. She felt as though she were floating. Floating over this living room, with the silver frame covered mantle, the ivy-patterned coach, the ribbed carpet that her mother couldn't seem to stop looking at. Over the plastic, manicured house with the red door, so far up that she couldn't hear the sole wind chime blowing in the wind.

"Jade," Caroline said. "I blanked. I'm—"

"My friend's waiting for me," Jade said. She walked toward the red door, turned the handle, looked back at her mother. "I shouldn't have come."

As the perfect red door closed behind her, Jade forced herself to watch Lily's car, refusing herself the chance to look back. Lily looked up and smiled, gave Jade a tentative thumbs-up. Jade shook her head, but Lily must not have seen it. As Jade buckled her seat belt, Lily beamed.

"It was her, wasn't it?"

The seat belt clicked in.

"How was she?"

Jade stared straight ahead. Lily hesitated, then thrust the key into the ignition. As the pickup truck rumbled out of the court, Jade allowed herself one look back at her mother's house. The sun was dimming for the day, and she could see inside the windows. Upstairs, Henry was bent close to the window, watching her. Downstairs, Carol's hand pressed against the window for a moment, and then she drew the curtain shut.

Chapter Seventeen: The Art of Losing

"I don't get it," Lily said as her truck rolled around the corner, exiting Willow Bend. "Why would she lie to him?"

"She's embarrassed by me," Jade said. She watched the fish stands fade away from them in the rearview mirror, replaced by a long stretch of yellow-lined concrete and gnarled sweetgums. "I'm part of her old life. She has a new one now."

"That can't be true. She's your mom."

"Not really," Jade said.

"Would you rather have not known, do you think?" Lily asked.

Trees rustled by the window. Jade didn't answer. As they passed the sign welcoming them back in to Paradise, she contemplated asking Lily to turn the car around. Not to bring it back to Willow Bend, but to keep driving down the stretch of road, putting as much swampy terrain between herself and Margaret and Caroline as possible.

"You can stay with me and my mom, if you want," Lily said as the sign slipped from view in the side mirror. "As long as you need to."

Jade nodded, her gaze still fixed on the rearview mirror. "Thank you," she said. "Seriously."

Lily turned to look at Jade and, turning back to the road, had to swerve away from an impending curb. The car pointing straight again, she spoke with her eyes fixed ahead. "Of course."

When they pulled into Lily's driveway, her mom was

sitting on the porch steps. She stood up when she saw them and ran toward the truck, waving erratically.

"Jesus," Lily said as she stopped the car. "What's her problem?"

Her mom jostled with Lily's door handle. Lily opened the door and her mother bent down to poke her head in. Jade noted the puffiness underneath her eyes, the way her breath shook as she looked directly at Jade. She'd been crying.

"Mom?" Lily's tone shifted. "What's wrong?"

Lily's mom ignored her, turning instead to Jade. She spoke as though she were making a concerted effort to speak slowly and calmly, but the words came out in a desperate, fast-paced clutter. "Honey, your grandma's sick. We need to get you to the hospital, now."

"What happened?" Jade asked as Lily's mom slid into the backseat and squeezed Jade's shoulder a bit too tightly.

"Doctor Schnell said a heart attack."

Jade could feel the very pit of her stomach. She could feel the blood beating into her forehead. And she could hear Lily's mom speaking as the car started up again and jolted out of the driveway, but she only registered snippets of it.

Doctor Schnell called an hour ago. Jade closed her eyes and saw herself lying in bed with Margaret, learning the names of the Greek gods and goddesses. *He said she's in the ICU, but I'm sure she'll be fine.* Opera music pounding the floors of the house. *Lily, tell your friend it'll be okay.* Searching the beach for conch shells, finding a stranded jellyfish, soft white gelatin absorbing the hot sand. *Mom, leave her alone.* Spaghetti and broken plate shards on the kitchen floor. Sauce speckled Margaret's ankles. *Jade, seriously, are you okay?*

The car passed the church, and Jade thought of Randy Banks' funeral. Randy Banks: not a passing friend, not an acquaintance—a man Margaret had loved and lived with. And Jade had judged her for mourning him. A tree with huge boughs flew past them. Jade remembered the feeling of sap on her palms, Margaret looking up at her, encouraging her to climb up another branch. A man walked by in an orange vest. Jade remembered the orange coat she'd lost on a school field trip, back in first grade. She saw Margaret sitting on the other end of the couch, reading her a poem by Elizabeth Bishop.

The art of losing isn't hard to master;
so many things seem filled with the intent
to be lost that their loss is no disaster.

The Paradise Hospital was roughly the size of Paradise Elementary School. There were only a handful of doctors and nurses, and so few rooms that patients were separated with sliding curtains. Lily and her mom flanked Jade as they walked down the hallway. Doctor Schnell was in front of the third door, speaking to a nurse who gave Jade a sympathetic glance as she stepped away.

"Where is she?" Jade asked, already moving towards the room. "Margaret Adelson, my grandma, where is she?"

"Wait," Doctor Schnell put his arm out to stop Jade. "We should talk first."

"In here?" Jade asked, leaning around the doorframe to try to catch a glimpse of Margaret. The bed was obscured by a sliding curtain.

"She's had a heart attack," Doctor Schnell said slowly. "A relatively small one, we think, but we're still assessing the state of her heart. For now, she needs to rest."

Jade exhaled. A relatively small heart attack didn't sound fatal. She walked past the doctor's outstretched arm, mumbling "I need to see her" under her breath.

Medicine was flowing from a hanging plastic sack into Margaret's arm, which hung limply across the hospital bed sheets. She was asleep, her dyed auburn bob spread across the pillow. Jade sat on the edge of the bed and put her hand on her grandmother's arm. She could see the roots of her grandmother's hair, devolving back into silvery gray at her temples and the top of her scalp. Jade felt like she was in a movie theater, watching a devastated granddaughter visit her grandmother. Separated from the scene entirely, eating popcorn and sipping on Coca-Cola.

"Grandma?"

Margaret's eyes twitched open, then widened. Her words slurred together as she cleared her throat and started to speak."Didyou findher?"

Jade nodded.

"I'm sorry," Margaret whispered. Her lips were pale, cracked, and they moved away from each other with difficulty, as if drawn together by a string.

"I know," Jade said. She squeezed her grandmother's hand and felt bone. "We'll talk about it later."

Margaret's lips shook open, but then she ran out of breath, took a long exhale, and sealed her lips and eyelids once again. Jade gripped her hand tighter and started to cry. She imagined Margaret sitting in the kitchen alone, staring at the ruined spaghetti on the floor, jazz still playing, melancholy, in the background. Jade's gut pounded with guilt. Out of the corner of her eye, she could see a young nurse watching her from the doorway for a moment, and then, thinking better of intruding on the moment, walking away.

A few more nurses had poked their heads into the room by the time Jade had stopped crying. She wanted to cry more, but her face felt too numb, so she just sat there, staring at Margaret's flickering eyelids. Eventually, Lily came in to check on her. She walked toward her slowly, as though Jade were the patient.

"Jade," she said after a long moment of hesitation. "I just spoke to the doctor."

"What?" Jade turned in her chair, and the plastic coating squeaked under her shifting weight. "Why? What did he say?"

"It's nothing to do with Margaret, don't worry," Lily said, her voice still pouring out like cold medicine into a clear cup, slow, sticky. "But—"

"What?" Jade stood up. "The tests came back, didn't they?"

"No," Lily said. "I'm sorry, I should've just said—they called your mom."

Jade sat back down. Margaret's snores permeated the room. Jade had never realized how deeply her grandmother snored; maybe the wind chimes were meant to disguise the sound, she thought detachedly.

"Doctor Schnell said she was on Margaret's form as second contact, next to you. Caroline was treated here a couple years ago, so Doctor Schnell had her information on file. When he couldn't reach you, he—he called her."

"She was treated here? For what?"

"Doctor Schnell wouldn't tell me. He just said she was on her way."

"She won't want to talk to her," Jade said, turning to her grandmother. "I don't know why she put her on her—on her file... she doesn't want to..." Jade started to cry again.

"I'm sorry, Jade." Lily lowered herself to Jade's level and took her hand, squeezed it. "I'm so sorry."

Jade nodded, sniffling. "Can you tell me when she's here?"

Lily nodded. And then she left, and it was just Jade and Margaret once more. Jade folded over herself, bending her head to rest on the bed next to Margaret's outstretched hand. The sounds of Margaret's snores rolled on like incoming waves, continual, reassuring. Jade fell asleep, and when she woke up, her mother's hand was on her shoulder.

Caroline's face hung over her, sympathetic. "I'm here," she said, as if she were only just realizing this herself.

Up close, Jade could see the thick swabs of concealer swiped across her mother's cheeks like silly putty, the raw parts of her lips shining under her dark red lipstick. She bit her lips, just like Jade did. Just like Margaret did.

Jade sat up, turned towards her grandmother. Margaret's eyelids flickered slightly every few seconds, creating the illusion that they might open wide at any moment.

"She's still asleep," Caroline said. "Maybe we should go outside."

"No," Jade said. "I'm staying with her."

Caroline hesitated, then nodded. She pulled up a chair next to Jade's. The chair legs squealed against the faux-marble floors. Jade looked back at Margaret, but her eyes were still twitching, mid-dream.

"I wonder what she's dreaming about," Caroline said softly. Her face was childlike as she watched her mother. Jade wished she could rub a makeup wipe across that face. What did she want to reveal? Her true mother, the mother she'd expected? This was her mother, this small, makeup-caked woman who hid her own daughter from her husband and sat on an ivy-webbed couch behind closed curtains, shooing away Girl Scouts all day.

"Does Fred know about me at all?" Jade said, still watching Margaret.

Maybe Margaret wasn't having a dream, but a nightmare. Maybe she was re-living Jade leaving her, her heart knotting itself, squeezing the air out of her lungs. Watching her, Jade felt as though she couldn't breathe.

Caroline's eyes were fixed on the IV drip, the drops of clear medicine flowing into her mother's veins. "No," she said finally. "He doesn't."

Jade nodded. "And your son?"

"Step-son," Caroline said quickly.

"He doesn't know," Jade said, her question morphing into a statement as it left her lips.

Caroline shook her head, pulling her chalky red lips in and looking down at the floor.

"Why did you come?"

"She's still my mother," Caroline said. "For everything she did to me, she's still my mother."

"Did to you?" Jade's voice curdled into a yell. She lowered her voice, turned and looked her mother in the eyes. "How can this be about you?"

"I'm sorry," Caroline whispered.

Jade expected an excuse, an explanation, but Caroline said nothing else. Once again, Jade couldn't breathe. Her heart seemed to be growing as it pounded, taking up the space where her lungs should have been.

"You didn't even try," Jade continued. She frowned, concentrated on breathing steadily as she spoke.

"We should have this talk later. You're tired. I'll get us some sandwich—"

"Why are you even here?"

"I'm her—" Caroline gestured to Margaret. She cut herself off and turned to Jade with the face of someone still convincing themselves. "I'm your mom."

Jade knew that she would cry if she spoke, so she simply shook her head.

Chapter Eighteen: Ham and Cheese Sandwiches

While Jade watched Margaret sleep, Caroline went to the hospital coffee corner and got them saran-wrapped sandwiches.

"Ham and cheese," she said as she handed Jade the damp, wrinkled bundle. "I hope that's okay?"

"I guess," Jade said, fully aware that this was her favorite sandwich. She started to unwrap the sandwich gingerly.

"Right," Caroline said. "I'll be outside if you need me."

Caroline started to sit up, and her chair creaked ominously. Margaret groaned and turned in her bed. She opened her eyes as if they'd been sealed shut for years.

Jade leaned forward, gripped Margaret's hand. "Can you hear me, Grandma?"

Margaret nodded, her eyes wide and disoriented like, those of a child, shaken from her nap.

"Mom?" Caroline whispered. "It's me."

Margaret's lips puckered, and her cheeks started to shake. Her eyes welled up. She pushed her arms down against the bed, tried to propel herself up. A nurse, watching from the hallway, ran in and helped her to sit up.

"It's alright, ma'am, it's alright. Your daughter and granddaughter are here."

Margaret was watching Caroline as if she were a flickering phantom at the end of her bed, but the nurse didn't notice. She fluffed the pillow behind Margaret's neck and left, pulling a curtain divider across the section of the room as she left. Jade watched the curtain sway for a moment, then hang still, limp. Wheels squeaked against the floor as another patient was brought into the room. Still, Margaret watched Caroline, her eyes slowly registering her daughter's face. Jade imagined that she was peeling back the effects of makeup and time, trying to find the girl she raised. The girl in the pink taffeta dress.

"Am I—" Margaret asked, tracing her fingers along the tubes attached to the inside of her elbow.

"No," Jade said, immediately understanding. "You're going to be okay."

"Then why are you here?" Margaret said, turning to Caroline. "Why did you come back?"

Caroline was silent, her face searching for sympathy.

"Why are you here?" Margaret repeated. Her breathing was shallow, as though her lungs could only afford to accept the air in small gulps.

"I—I don't know," Caroline said. She had crossed her hands against her lap, and they shook as she spoke. "You put me on your contact list. I thought—"

"Your hair," Margaret whispered. "It changed."

Caroline nodded. She stood up slowly, walked to the bed and sat down on it, just next to Margaret.

"You're different," Margaret said simply. Jade watched them, their eyes locked together in a shared vortex of concealed emotions and time, and suddenly felt estranged from both of them.

"I'm clean," Caroline said. "Two years now."

Margaret's face crumpled into itself. She was smiling, but tears slid down her cheeks. She reached out and cupped Caroline's cheek. "I knew you could, if you just—"

"Why then?" Jade interrupted. "Why two years ago?"

"Fred," Caroline said, still watching Margaret. "My husband. We met three years ago, and he went through every second of it with me. Paid for my treatment—at this hospital, actually—that's why they had my phone number on file."

Margaret smiled even more broadly. Jade, meanwhile, felt sick. "Why was Fred enough?" she asked softly, looking down at her shoes.

Caroline finally turned around and looked at her daughter. Her bottom lip was shaking. "It's not like that," she said.

Jade's gaze shifted to the cracks on the floor.

"It's not a question of enough, Jade, please believe me."

"Okay," Jade said. She looked up at Caroline, willed her to look her in the eyes. "But why could you do it for him, but not for me?"

Caroline opened her mouth to respond, but Margaret interrupted her.

"I was wrong," Margaret said. Her voice grated, like sand pooling in the wake of a strong tide. Her gaze shifted between Caroline and Jade, both watching her in surprise. "I was wrong," she repeated. "Caroline, I should've tried harder."

Caroline grabbed Margaret's hand, and Margaret curled her other hand on top, holding on with two hands as if Caroline might leave before she could say what she wanted to say.

"I should have said that a long time ago," Margaret continued. "Like Randy wanted me to."

"Randy?" Caroline turned to Jade. "The one who helped you find me?"

"We met the first day Jade and I got here," Margaret said. "At Gil's, actually. We got engaged six months later." Margaret smiled softly, her cheeks shining.

"Where is he?" Caroline asked, looking around the room as if she could've missed him.

"He's gone now," Margaret whispered. "And I wasn't

with him when he went. Because I didn't want to believe him when he said I was doing the wrong thing. He hated the lies."

Caroline frowned, and Jade realized that she still didn't know.

"I told Jade that you were a treasure hunter." Margaret's face fell.

"A what?" Caroline turned to Jade. "You thought I was a... treasure hunter?"

Jade could feel herself growing defensive. She didn't want to be mad at Margaret, with the drooping bags of medication plugged into her veins, her face already drained of energy. But she couldn't stop thinking about the pile of letters in her desk at home. She could hear them piling against each other, paper falling on paper, crowding the drawer until there was no room for anything else—

"I'm checking on Lily," Jade announced. "I'll be back," she added, seeing the fear on Margaret's face.

She breathed jaggedly as she walked out of the room. She could hear Caroline whispering something to Margaret, but she didn't care what they were saying. She had always imagined an emptiness inside herself, where Caroline was supposed to be but wasn't. But now she realized that this place was not empty, but full: full of anger and confusion and a desire to face-plant into a pillow and scream. Jade imagined a constellation, a burst of light. She wanted to punch something, an urge she had never felt before.

Lily stood up when she saw Jade coming. Her mother was asleep in the chair next to her. Jade scanned the room until she found a clock: it was already 5 o'clock. On Lily's other side, Jade noted with surprise, sat Al and Linda. Linda was flipping through a magazine, but she looked up sympathetically when she saw Jade moving toward them.

"How is she?" Lily asked.

"Can we go on a drive?"

"Where?"

"Doesn't matter. Please."

Lily turned to Linda and said something to her. Linda nodded gravely, grabbing Lily's arm before she turned away. "Let us know if we can do anything," she said, looking back and forth between Lily and Jade.

"Thanks," Lily said, and her voice was softer than Jade had ever heard it get, at least around Linda and Al.

Out in the hospital parking lot, Jade walked quickly to Lily's car. She passed a woman in the final throes of pregnancy, her husband clutching onto her forearm as she walked slowly and breathed rapidly. A nurse ran out with a wheelchair and rolled the woman into the building, the husband jogging to keep up.

The car door slammed behind Jade. Lily sat down next to her, but didn't put her key in the ignition. "Do you want to stay here?" she asked.

"Can we go to Gil's?"

Lily gave Jade an odd look as she started the car. Jade wondered where Lily had expected she would want to go. The beach, maybe. It would be therapeutic, listening to the water melting into the brim of the ocean, over and over, accepting that the hunt was over, that it had been no more real than the jewelry under Mr. Werner's petunias or the gold stains under her mother's feet. But Jade had one move left to make before she gave up hope. And, based on what Margaret had just said, the last step was at Gil's Sandwich Shop.

Chapter 19: Everything

The bell chimed ominously as Lily and Jade walked into the shop. Gil came out of the kitchen briskly. His hands drummed against the counter as he spoke. "Hello, ladies. The usual?"

"Sure," Lily said hesitantly. She was watching Jade, likely wondering whether she was bordering on a nervous breakdown. "Jade, let's sit."

Jade stayed standing. She met Gil in the eyes and refused to look down. If Randy Banks had left his treasure here, Gil would have to know.

"Gil," she said levelly. She couldn't believe she could talk so normally, like her grandmother wasn't in the hospital and her mother wasn't a liar. "Did Randy Banks come here a lot?"

"A lot? Man was half my business," Gil said. "Sandwiches, all day long. It's a wonder he survived so long." Gil stopped. "That wasn't funny. I shouldn't have said that."

"It's okay, Gil," Lily said. "Jade, let's sit."

"Did you ever see him here with my grandmother?" Jade continued, ignoring Gil's reddening neck and cheeks.

Gil's mouth twisted uncomfortably. His hands tapped against the counter with increasing speed and force.

Lily looked back and forth between him and Jade. "What's going on, Jade?" she asked.

"You did," Jade prompted Gil, ignoring her friend. "Where did they sit?"

Gil gestured to the booth in the corner of the room and, without another word, disappeared behind the kitchen door. Lily gave Jade a concerned look as it swung behind him.

"Jade?" she asked slowly. "What are you—"

Jade started toward the booth. Her heart was pounding, climbing up her throat, but her mind felt unusually clear. She scanned the booth for a few seconds, tied her hair back, and slid in the gap between the back of the booth and the wall behind it. Lily watched her silently, her lips slightly parted in confusion.

"It would be here," Jade said, bending over as far as she could and sliding her hand against the red vinyl. It was cracked and peeling with age, but when Jade's hand moved to the bottom right corner, she felt a spot even more worn down than the rest. There was a hole the size of her fist, and when Jade stuck her hand into it, she felt a slight prick: the corner of a piece of paper.

"Jade," Lily said firmly. "Gil's going to be out with our sandwiches. Shouldn't we… sit down?"

Lily was embarrassed, Jade realized. She thought she was having a breakdown of sorts. And Jade would feel embarrassed and nervous, if she wasn't so sure she was right. She clipped the paper between two fingers and wiggled her hand until it came out. She held it up to Lily victoriously. It was a letter, and when Jade flipped it around to see what it said, she saw her name. She recognized the curling scrawl as Randy Banks'. Without moving from her spot between the booth and wall, Jade ripped it open.

Dear Jade,

"What does it say?" Lily asked impatiently. "Is it Randy Banks?"

Dear Jade,

I went back and forth about how to give this to you. Writing it down in my will would've been simple enough. But then I remembered how much you loved treasure hunts as a little girl. Do you remember? I used to hide things—my watch, a spare dollar, a piece of candy—and give you 5 clues. You got it every time.

Jade suddenly remembered the crumple of a piece of candy in her fist. She remembered a feeling of elation as she pulled it out from beneath a mattress. She'd always wondered, looking back at that memory, how the candy had gotten there.

Even if you don't remember me by now, I thought you might remember the treasure hunting. I hope you enjoyed it, Jade. I wish I could watch you piece it all together, like I used to, but I think it would hurt too much, seeing you and knowing that it's too late for me to come back into your life. The truth is, I still love you like my own daughter. That's why I'm leaving you and your grandmother with everything I have. The lawyer will come soon, with all the nitty gritty bits, but here's the gist: I want you two to have my house and everything in it. My books, my maps, everything I have I leave to you. I'm sorry to say I don't have any gold, but I do have a fair amount of money put away, and all that goes to you, too.

I've attached a second letter in this envelope for your grandmother. Please make sure she gets it. And, Jade, remember, no matter what happens, that she loves you very much. More than I ever thought possible.

Love,
Randy

Jade's eyes moved so quickly across the letter that she wasn't sure if she'd absorbed everything. She read it again, only half-conscious of Lily staring at her, waiting for an explanation. She was reading the second paragraph, the bit about the house and the books and the money, for the third time when Gil came out of the kitchen carrying two sandwiches on paper plates.

"Oh, thank God above," Gil said when he saw them, Jade sandwiched behind the booth, Lily watching with her hands on her hips. They both turned to him. "I thought I was going to give it all away for a second there."

"You knew?" Jade winced as she pulled herself out from behind the booth.

"Of course I knew," Gil said proudly. His voice softened sadly as he added, "He told me the day before he died. Shoved that letter in and said, 'Gil, you've been a good friend and an honest man to me. Make sure Jade Adelson gets that letter in the end, but don't give her any clue it's there unless it looks like she's given up."

"What does it say, Jade?" Lily asked. "Is there any..."

"There's no actual treasure," Jade said, rubbing her thumbs against the paper as if to make sure it was real. "But he left me everything."

"Everything?"

"The house, the money," Jade looked up at Lily. "Everything."

Chapter Twenty: Cracks in the Ceiling

"I don't understand," Caroline said abrasively. She was eating chocolate pudding out of a plastic cup, carefully puffing out her lips as she drew the spoon to her mouth, so as to protect her lipstick. "Why wouldn't he just tell you? That seems like a weird prank to play."

Jade ignored her mother. She was watching her grandmother's reaction. Margaret's face hadn't moved in minutes, ever since Jade handed her the two letters from Randy Banks. She'd read them slowly, tracing a finger across the writing as if it were tangible, touchable. Finally, she closed her eyes and breathed out, flattening the letter against the palm of her hand.

"There must be someone else," Margaret said hollowly. "We didn't talk for years."

"This is what he said he wanted, Grandma," Jade said. She squeezed her hand, wondering what the second letter had said.

"But I hurt him," Margaret said. She leaned forward into Jade's shoulder as she started to cry, her entire body shaking under the paper-thin hospital gown. She shook for a long time, and then she lay back on the bed and stared at the ceiling. "I don't want the house," she said suddenly.

"You can sell it," Caroline suggested.

"No. That's not right."

"We'll figure it out later," Jade said, a plan already forming in her mind. "In the meantime, I saw Doctor Schnell on my way in here. He has some good news." Jade smiled down at her grandmother. "You're good to go."

"Oh, thank god," Caroline said. She rubbed her forehead absent-mindedly. "I'll have to go soon. Fred's expecting me."

"We'll need a ride home," Jade said, looking up from her grandmother. "Lily's gone home with her family."

Caroline's lower lip hung in hesitation, and Jade silently swore to herself that she would never forgive her mother if she left them there.

"Of course," Caroline said finally.

When Doctor Schnell came in to echo the good news, he handed Caroline a stapled packet of recommendations: meal plans, exercise and activity restrictions, medications. Caroline flipped through it mindlessly while the doctor spoke, clearly not paying much mind to its contents. She handed the packet to Jade as soon as he left the room. Then he left the room and a nurse came in. She lifted Margaret's bed and helped her transfer into a wheelchair, with a hammock leather seat and two alarmingly scuffed-up wheels. The nurse pushed her down the hallway, and Jade and Caroline followed.

Jade watched her mother out of the corner of her eye as they walked. She wanted her to come closer, to put her arm around her. But Caroline's eyes were set straight ahead. Jade wondered if she was counting the cracks in the floor, like Jade always did. They reached Caroline's car, the wheelchair screeching and twisting across the broken concrete, and Caroline helped the nurse lift Margaret into the backseat.

"I could really do this by my—" Margaret's words were cut off as the nurse shut the car door. Jade smiled at Margaret's tone. She could already tell that enforcing the doctor's instructions would be a full-time job.

As Jade scooted into the backseat, she noticed that Margaret was still looking wan, her veins visible even in the fading afternoon light. She rested her head against the window and didn't talk throughout the drive. Caroline didn't say much either. Every once in a while, Jade would look at the rearview mirror and see her mother's mouth open. She expected some kind of question. *What's school like? Do you have a boyfriend?* But then Caroline would close her lips again, and Jade would go back to browsing potential topics of conversation.

It started to rain just before they reached the house. Jade was relieved; the sounds of raindrops plopping against the hood of the car was far better than the silence preceding it. Then they reached the house and had to wheel Margaret across the unpaved driveway, up the porch steps, and into the house. Jade went to fetch the key that was stored under the largest rock in the garden and found that it was already caked in wet dirt. She wiped it off on her jeans, unlocked the door, and wheeled her grandmother inside. Margaret was shivering terribly. Jade helped her onto the couch and turned on the TV. She assumed that Caroline was standing behind her all the while, but when she turned around, it was just her and Margaret in the living room.

"No," Jade whispered to herself. She walked quickly to the door, but Caroline's car was still there. Caroline, on the other hand, was not inside of it.

Jade found her mother in the attic, sitting on Jade's bed with her eyes were fixed on the ceiling.

"I used to be scared of cracks in the ceiling," Caroline said as Jade walked in. "This is your room?"

"Yeah."

Caroline nodded meekly. She patted the bed, and Jade sat down next to her.

"You know when you start wearing makeup," Caroline said. "And after a while you get sick of having to put it on every day, but everyone's so used to seeing you in it, and you're so used to being the person you are when you wear it, that you just keep it on?"

"Margaret doesn't let me wear makeup," Jade said. She watched rain drops slither down her window, colliding with each other like rivers feeding into an ocean.

"No," Caroline said, looking back up at the ceiling. "She didn't let me, either."

The rain was hypnotizing. Jade wondered why new rain drops followed the same patterns as the ones before them.

"What I'm trying to say," Caroline said, finally looking down from the ceiling. "Is that I tried to remake myself after what happened with your grandmother. And now I'm used to the makeup I wear."

"The makeup being that you pretend not to have a daughter?"

"No," Caroline said quickly. "Pretending not to have been such a, well, a bad mother, I guess."

"Where does Fred think you are right now?"

"He knows I went to the hospital," Caroline said earnestly. "I told him I was visiting an old friend. Broke her ankle playing tennis."

"That's an elaborate lie."

"I can't—" Caroline stopped. She closed her eyes. "He can't know about you, Jade. I'm sorry, but I just can't tell him."

Jade watched the window. She imagined Caroline walking back into her house, kissing Fred on the cheek, telling him about the friend from the country club who landed on her ankle wrong. Would she give him a name for the friend? How in-depth did her lies go?

"It's not that he's a bad man," Caroline said, as if Jade cared what kind of man he was. "It's just that—well, when I went into the hospital, he thought I told him everything. He has a big thing against holding things back—"

"Lying," Jade corrected her.

"Lying," Caroline conceded, looking up at her daughter guiltily. "If he knew that after everything I put him through, I wasn't telling him so much… if he knew I was such an awful mother…" Caroline breathed in sharply, her eyes darting to the ceiling. "I know he'd leave me."

For a moment, Jade felt a glimpse of pity for the woman sitting on her bed. She wondered, as she had ever since Margaret told her about her mother, why her father had left. But she also knew that if she brought this up, she was only giving Caroline another window to excuse herself, to build up a wall of pity instead of admitting that she was in the wrong.

Jade got up and walked to her desk. She fished inside until she'd found the packet of letters. Placing them in front of Caroline, she muttered, "I had things I needed to talk about."

Caroline opened the first letter, written when Jade got into the Dolphins reading group in first grade. In second grade, a story Jade had written about treasure hunting with Caroline. In fourth grade, Jade ranted about her math teacher, and how much Margaret's egg sandwiches stunk. Caroline read them silently. Every once in a while, she would pause to look up at Jade. When she'd gotten through half of them, she buried her face in her hands.

"I really, really thought," she said. "I was doing the right thing."

The rain outside started to subside, and the house grew quieter. Jade could hear the mutterings of the TV coming from the living room.

"Do you still," Caroline inhaled sharply. "Would you still want to write to me? I could do that."

"What would Fred say, seeing letters from me?"

Caroline hesitated. From the living room, Jade could hear Margaret coughing. She stood up abruptly and moved toward the staircase.

"I'll write to you," Caroline said weakly as Jade paused on the second step.

Jade looked back at her mother. Seeing her there, sitting on the bed where Jade had slept her whole life, from the ages of three to sixteen, felt wrong somehow. Like a dream that she would think back on for weeks on end, always wondering how it would've ended if she hadn't woken up in a cold sweat. She would learn the end to this some other time, she decided as she heard Margaret emit another wheezing cough.

"We'll talk later," Jade said. "Grandma," she called out. "Are you okay?"

In the living room, Jade sat next to her grandmother and leaned on her shoulder. They sat there in silence, Caroline still upstairs, Jade listening to the steady thumping of her grandmother's heart. Margaret's breathing was shattered, disjointed, as if her lungs were too tired to fully expand. Doctor Schnell said she had a minor cold on top of everything else, that the best thing she could do was rest.

"Is she still here?" Margaret asked. Her eyes were closed. Jade noticed that one of her eyelashes was paler than the rest.

"In my room," Jade said.

Margaret put her hand over Jade's. Within minutes, her heavy breathing had lengthened into a series of snores. Jade closed her eyes too, certain that she would soon stand up and speak to Caroline. She wondered what her mother was doing in her room. There wasn't much to look at. Was she still watching the crack on the ceiling? Was she planning a speech for Fred, or wondering how best to escape the house without hurting Jade's feelings? Jade's body suddenly felt very heavy against the collapsing couch.

When Jade woke up, Margaret was reading a poetry book on the edge of the couch. She whispered along as she read. It was nighttime, and the only light in the house came from the lamp above them. Margaret's head created a gray shadow over the stark white pages. It wavered as she turned the pages.

"Is she still here?" Jade sat up, stretching her legs out in front of her.

"No," Margaret said, looking up from her book. "She said she'd be back soon, though. To check on us."

"I doubt it."

"I think," Margaret paused. "I think she's going to try."

Jade nodded and Margaret turned back to her book. Jade closed her eyes again and listened to Margaret's fingers trace the coarse pages, flip them over, hesitate, and return to tracing the lines.

Chapter Twenty-One: Piles

Randy Banks' lawyer visited two days after Margaret and Jade had left the hospital with letters from Randy Banks. Jade was sitting on the porch when he came, catching up on her summer homework. She guided him back to the living room, where Margaret was still couch-bound.

"I'm sorry to come so late," he said, sitting down next to Margaret on the living room couch. "But Randy specifically asked that I got the go-ahead from a Mr. Gil Portman before I called. I'm assuming you know why?"

Margaret nodded. Jade leaned a pitcher of lemonade over a tall glass and poured silently while she listened.

"Anyway, now that that's done, I have some news for you," the lawyer continued. He unfolded a crisp sheet of paper and carefully laid it on the table, in front of Margaret.

Margaret swallowed as she read the number at the bottom of the page. "That can't—is that right?" she asked, looking up at the lawyer.

He nodded.

The lawyer walked them through the mound of paperwork, but in the end, it wasn't so complicated. Just as Randy had said, everything he had went to her and Margaret. The house, the bank accounts, and an impressive number of investments. There was a section of savings put aside for Jade's college fund, but the rest was, as the lawyer put it, "no strings attached."

"What about his cousin?" Margaret asked. "It doesn't

seem right that she gets nothing."

"That's another thing I wanted to talk to you about," the lawyer said. "Randy Banks doesn't have a cousin. Neither of his parents had siblings. After that episode at the funeral, our firm went through all the paperwork we could find. No trace of her. Our best guess is that Ms. Eleanor Banks is Ms. Eleanor Something-Else, and when she read Randy's obituary in the *Paradise Sun* and heard the rumors about his gold, she put together a whole new persona for herself."

"That's terrible," Margaret muttered.

"Thankfully," the lawyer said. "There was no treasure—just a will. A will that very clearly says that everything will be left to you."

The next day, Jade and Lily walked to the library to break the news to Ms. Healey. Her hair was up in curlers when they came in. She jolted at the sight of them, her hands flying up to her hair. Her fingers moved deftly to pull the ringlets out of their turquoise casings.

"It's fine, Ms. Healey," Lily said, holding back her laughter. "We're not the paparazzi."

Ms. Healey's eyebrows lowered. "Ha, ha," she said slowly, settling back into her chair. "What do you girls want?"

"The library is overflowing," Jade said, gesturing towards the shelves of books, compressed into stacks that were inches away from touching the ceiling.

"Talk to the manager," Ms. Healey said sarcastically, rolling one of her curlers back into her hair.

"Jade and her grandmother want to offer you a new space," Lily said. "Would you be interested?"

Ms. Healey blew sharply on her freshly polished nails as she looked back and forth between the two girls. Her gaze settled on Jade. "You're serious? Where?"

The night before, Jade pitched her plan to Margaret.

The house would go to the library. It would be filled with the contents of the previous library, but also with the maps and poetry anthologies that Margaret said the house was already filled with. Some of the money Randy had left them would go towards fixing the pier and naming it after him. Jade was particularly proud of this addition, and Margaret started to cry when she suggested it. Jade paused until her grandmother had calmed down, and then she proposed the part of her plan that excited her the most.

"And finally," she had said, wishing she could orchestrate some kind of drumroll. "We can travel to all the places you told me about."

She pulled out a list she'd written that afternoon, just after the lawyer left. She'd poured over the letters she'd written to her mother, each addressed to a different country. "Brazil, Costa Rica, China, Japan, France, Scotland—"

"Jade," Margaret interrupted. "That's a wonderful plan, but we really should save. And neither of us have ever been out of the country—"

"Exactly," Jade said. "Grandma, I don't think Randy wanted us to save his money. If he wanted to be practical about it, he would've had his will sent straight to us."

Ms. Healey agreed immediately to the deal, but it took a few weeks for it to come to fruition. Margaret was still on bed-rest, and she insisted on being there to sort through Randy's things before the house was handed over. And so, almost a month after their plan had originally formed, they drove down the road to the Banks estate together. Jade drove hesitantly, braking too quickly and then too slowly, secretly fearful of giving her grandmother another heart attack. They stopped in front of the house, the car jolting forward a bit as Jade stomped on the brake. Margaret sat there for a few moments, her eyes fluttering upwards as she breathed in and out. Jade, meanwhile, was watching the sunlight flicker through the scraggly trees surrounding the home when she saw a glimpse of cherry red bordering the side of the house. She stepped out of the car wordlessly and walked around the wrap-around balcony. There it was: the glinting red paint, the cheetah print seats, the frozen dancer.

"Grandma," Jade called as she walked back to the front of the house. "We might have to—"

The car was empty, the screen door of the house swung open and creaking slightly in the summer wind. Jade muttered a curse under her breath as she walked in after her grandmother.

She found herself in an entryway not unlike the backroom of Weird Al's. The Persian rug was decked with dust and stacks of overflowing boxes, whose cardboard edges were splitting with the weight of their contents. The walls were covered with maps, some framed, some jabbed into the drywall with colorful thumbtacks. And on the grand staircase leading down to the entryway, bath-robed and wide-eyed, was Ms. Eleanor Banks, or whatever her real name was. Margaret, standing at the bottom of the entryway, was looking up at her in confusion.

"I don't understand," Margaret was saying. "How did you get in?"

"I don't know who you think you are," Ms. Banks said, pulling her robe tighter around her body. "Just barging into my cousin's home like this."

"Grandma," Jade said, walking to stand beside Margaret. "This is Eleanor… Banks. The woman the lawyer told us about."

Ms. Banks' eyes narrowed when she saw Jade. "We've met before," she said, her facade fading.

"We have."

"What are you doing here?" Ms. Banks' face was reddening. Her moccasins were planted firmly on the stair.

"Randy Banks left this house to my grandmother. The question is," Jade said, glancing at Margaret, who still seemed to be processing Ms. Banks. "What are you doing here? Did you break in?"

"Wh—" Ms. Banks swallowed deeply. "You're lying. I should call the police!"

"Go ahead," Margaret said, regaining her composure. "That'll save us some trouble."

Ms. Banks glared at her for a moment, hesitated, and then turned and ran up the stairs.

"What on Earth is she doing?" Margaret asked, turning to Jade with a bemused expression.

Ms. Banks yelled down at them from the second floor. There were thumps in between her words, and then the sounds of zippers being sealed.

"I—*THUMP*— never experienced anything like it—*THUMP*— disrespectful—unbelievable…"

There was the sound of wheels rolling across the floor, and then Ms. Banks was standing in front of them again, two large suitcases framing her sides like diligent basset hounds.

"It's not worth it," Ms. Banks said, straining to lower her suitcases down the staircase, stair by stair. Jade wondered for a moment whether she should help her, but then remembered Al's face when she left the bar, purse filled with maps.

"I'm sorry you didn't find the treasure, Ms. Banks," Jade said coyly.

Ms. Banks looked up at Jade in shock. One of the suitcases slipped, skipping the last two steps and landing face-down on the floor. Jade leaned over and lifted it upright.

"There is no treasure," Ms. Banks said. She was searching Jade's face. "Why do you say that?"

Jade looked back at her silently, fighting an urge to laugh. She knew she was being mean, but the image of Al persisted in the back of her mind.

"You didn't find it," Ms. Banks whispered. "You can't have. I would've seen you." She turned to Margaret, whose face was just as stony as Jade's. "I have searched—" Ms. Banks inhaled dramatically. "Every inch of this place. There is *no* treasure."

"Of course not," Margaret said. "Why would there be treasure here?"

Ms. Banks looked back and forth between granddaughter and grandmother. For a moment, it seemed as if she might run outside and start madly digging holes. But then she closed her eyes and inhaled again.

"I am leaving," Ms. Banks said. She paused, and then shook her head. "No, I am leaving."

Margaret and Jade went out to the porch and waved her goodbye. Once the cherry red car had turned out of the forested drive, Jade folded over laughing. Margaret smiled slightly, and then turned back to the house.

"Come back in, Jade," Margaret said. "We have work to do."

They worked room by room, sorting Randy's things into three piles: landfill, library, and keep. Margaret worked slowly, stopping to look at everything before inevitably deciding to keep it. Jade, meanwhile, worked as quickly as she could. It felt invasive, this practice of picking apart the things of a man she couldn't remember. Everything in this room had been valuable to him, valuable enough to keep. She felt like a vulture, tossing Christmas ornaments, leather diaries, and high school yearbooks alike into trash bags. Every once in a while, Margaret would abandon her section of the room to look into Jade's trash bag. She would pull half of its contents out, sniffle slightly, and put them in the "keep" pile. Jade said nothing, as much as she wanted to remind her grandmother of the square footage of their home.

In the living room, Jade paused at the piano. She ran

her fingers over the aged ivory keys, laid over each other like crooked teeth. She pushed down on the last key and a sharp, discordant noise filled the room. When Jade sat down and let the sound fill her, she noticed that the piano seat was wobbly. She stood up. There was a latch on the side, and when she pulled it up, it revealed a hollow inside, filled with photo albums. Jade pulled a leather-bound album from the bench and stared at the cover for a moment. She looked towards the entryway, where Margaret was turned away from her, shuffling through a book. Slowly, Jade opened the photo album to the first page.

A younger version of herself smiled up at her. Jade recognized herself from the pictures on Margaret's fridge. She was wearing a pink polka-dotted swimsuit, her chubby toddler legs caked in sand. Her hair was curly; Margaret still complained about having had to tame that hair. And next to her, one hand on her curly-haired head, the other extended toward the camera in an open-palmed wave, was Randy Banks.

Jade turned the page, hungry for more pictures. On the next page, she was sitting on Randy's knee, eating her fourth birthday cake. Then she was on a carousel, gripping a golden pole attached to a chipping painted pony. She was laughing, she was crying, she was eating spaghetti, drinking milk from a plastic blue cup. In some of the pictures, Margaret stood next to or behind her, either looking down at Jade lovingly or giving the camera a glare of mock-anger. In others, Randy sat with them. He was smiling in all of the pictures, Jade noticed as she flipped to the last page of the album.

There, a crinkled piece of yellow construction paper had been wedged behind the plastic sheeting. On it was a picture, drawn in cracking veins of crayon, of three people: a child and two parents, based on their respective heights. Jade stared at this page the longest. She wished she could remember having drawn it. More than that, she wished she could remember Randy's reaction when he first saw it. Had he smiled, like he did in the pictures, his whole face expanding? Had he hugged her, drawn her close, told her he loved her? It seemed so odd, that this man could have loved her, could have been part of her family, and yet she had no recollection of him.

Jade closed the photo album. She was reaching for a framed picture of her and Margaret curled up in Jade's bed when she saw something that made her breath catch. It was a cardboard children's book, the kind found in a grocery store aisle. It was worth ninety-nine cents, according to the sticker plastered to it, yet Jade could suddenly remember it as the most valuable thing to her as a child. *Treasure Hunter's Guide*, the book's title read in bold, golden letters.

There was a picture of a little girl with a shovel, digging into the edge of the ocean. She was wearing a striped red and white shirt and a pirate's hat. Jade couldn't remember what the story was about, when she had read it, or who had read it to her, but she remembered looking at that cover page: at the little girl on the beach with the flashy shovel. She remembered thinking that this was the greatest story in the world. And, looking back at Margaret, sorting through a stack of magazines in the hallway, she could tell that this story had meant a lot to her grandmother, too.

Made in the USA
Monee, IL
12 June 2020

33468444R00080